Kneeling beside him, she put her hand on his forehead and saw the mark on her finger from the absent ring. The reminders of her past life.

Rolland held her until she was still. "Besides liking that you're blocking the sun, I would really like to kiss you."

His lips greeted hers in a kiss that defined perfection in its simplicity. There was a knowing about the way his mouth moved over hers, an assuredness in how his head tilted, and hers dropped to the side and back to accept his mouth and tongue, that made her know this wouldn't be the last time. That thought brought reality screeching back.

She planted both her hands against his chest and moved herself away.

"Melanie?"

"Wait. I need a minute." All of her senses began to work again and she heard birds caw. Squirrels hustled about their business and a deer ran past heading east.

Rolland got closer and though she didn't want to, she had to stop him.

Dear Reader,

This is my inaugural book for Silhouette Special Edition, so I thought I should introduce myself. I am Carmen Green and I've been a writer since the mid-nineties. I love writing funny, offbeat novels, but I have a serious side too, so you'll never really know what to expect. I love learning, flowers, family, friends and food. I never go on loops, but I don't mind talking to people, doing interviews or appearing at conferences. I love traveling and experiencing new things. I have great friends in this business and those that know me well know that I'm funny, straightforward and honest.

This book is quite special to me. Traumatic Brain Injury is a very serious condition, and for those that suffer from this condition and their families it is often life-altering. My prayers and thoughts go out to all of those who continue the battle to improve their lives and the lives of those affected by TBI. I try to reply to all of my readers. My e-mail address is carmengreen1201@gmail.com, and my Web site is www.authorcarmengreen.com.

I look forward to a career with Silhouette Special Edition and hearing from all of you.

Peace and blessings,

Carmen Green

THE HUSBAND SHE COULDN'T FORGET

CARMEN GREEN

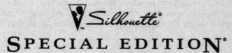

SPECIAL EDITION®

Published by Silhouette Books

America's Publisher of Contemporary Romance

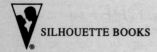

SILHOUETTE BOOKS

ISBN-13: 978-0-373-65480-2

Recycling programs
for this product may
not exist in your area.

THE HUSBAND SHE COULDN'T FORGET

Printed in U.S.A.

Books by Carmen Green

Silhouette Special Edition
The Husband She Couldn't Forget #1998

Kimani Romance
This Time for Good #90
The Perfect Solitaire #143

CARMEN GREEN

was born in Buffalo, NY, and had plans to study law before becoming a published author. While raising her three children, she wrote her first book on legal pads and transcribed it onto a computer on weekends before selling it in 1993. Since that time she has sold more than thirty novels and novellas, and is proud that one of her books was made into a TV movie in 2001, *Commitments,* in which she had a cameo role.

In addition to writing full-time, Carmen is now a mom of four, and lives in the Southeast. You can contact Carmen at www.carmengreen.blogspot.com or carmengreen1201@yahoo.com.

This book is dedicated to the U.S. Military,
and to Lori Bryant Woolridge and Nina Foxx,
two of the women along with myself
who founded the Femme Fantastik Tour.

It's been a humbling experience traveling to bases
and speaking to the soldiers and their families. I became
interested in the subject of Traumatic Brain Injury
because of an injury to a soldier, and I have a healthy
respect for all that they and their families must endure on
the path to recovery. I'm very proud of our soldiers,
and I hope to see you all again soon.

Prologue

Melanie stood on the top step of her Atlanta, Georgia, home and wondered how any woman in her right mind could be wearing stockings in this kind of June heat. The tall black woman who'd just rung her doorbell smelled faintly of cigarettes and looked as if she needed one bad.

An odd expression crossed her face, and Melanie looked at her own left hand and jerked it behind her back, embarrassed. She was still holding the Not Pregnant test stick from the pregnancy test she'd just taken, and her flush of disappointment sizzled into nothingness under the bright noon sun.

"I'm sorry, I just heard the door a second ago," Melanie said, pocketing the apparatus.

"Mrs. Melanie Bishop?"

"Yes, that's me."

Regret passed over the woman's face before she tapped Melanie's arm with a large manila envelope. "You've been served."

Hubert, Boyle and Stein. *Divorce attorneys*. She'd heard whispers about them in the ladies locker room at the country club her husband had insisted they join. They were the best. Or the worst. Depending on which side of the table you were on.

Her smile felt parched and false.

The woman took the winding steps down to the sidewalk in a hurry but sensing no threat, slowed down as she walked to her old grayish-looking Civic and got in. The car rumbled to life, but she didn't pull off.

Melanie stared at the envelope, knowing, but not wanting to know, why Deion was having her served.

The massive front door was blue. Deion wasn't fond of blue, but he hadn't said he hated blue. She could've changed it. Would've, had she known.

Maybe they shouldn't have compromised on the Porsche he'd wanted, and should have gotten it instead of the Lexus SUV.

But where would he put the baby when they had one?

That had been her argument.

Maybe he'd gotten tired of her arguments for everything.

Maybe Deion hated—

"Melanie?"

"Yes?" she said, looking around, unsure of who was calling her. It was the process server.

The woman had leaned over the passenger seat and was looking out the window. "You got a mama?" she called up to her.

"She died seven years ago." What an odd question coming from a stranger.

"A sister or best friend?"

"A friend." Him. Only him.

"Go in your house and call her right now. Okay?"

"Okay." Melanie turned the knob and put her shoulders into pushing the heavy door open. "Thank you."

"You're welcome."

Inside the house, her sneakers made *hush, hush* sounds on the nearly black hardwood floors and not for the first time, she felt as if the cool silence was mocking her. She'd only agreed to this house because she'd thought they'd fill it with children. But they'd been trying for five years and she didn't need telepathy to tell her that the papers in her hand were her expiration notice.

"Dial Deion's cell phone," she said aloud to the voice-activated system that controlled everything in the house.

She walked to their bedroom to Deion's closet and didn't notice more than the usual amount of clothes gone.

Deion was in New York at a conference for portfolio managers. She could hear his cell ringing, then roll over to voice mail. She sat on the end of their bed.

"This is Deion Bishop. I'm making deals happen, and if you're ready, I'll make them happen for you. Leave your name and number." His voice was still sexy after seven years of being together. She hadn't tired of it. Would never.

"Honey, we need to talk," she said, injecting a smile into her voice. "There has to be some way we can make this work. We can talk about anything. Please call me here at home. I love you. Goodbye. End call."

Two weeks after she was served, Melanie slid her maid's paycheck through the crack in the front door, but wouldn't open it all the way. "I don't need you this week, Juanita. I'm just not feeling well and I don't want you to catch my germs."

"Mrs. Bishop, I clean two times a week, every week for five years. Mr. Bishop says so. He doesn't like his bathroom with any dirt. I'm coming in."

"No!" Melanie swallowed her tears. "Mr. Bishop isn't here right now, so there's no need to worry about his bathroom. Here, I'll pay you for the entire month. I'll call you when I need you. Thank you, Juanita."

"Mrs. Bishop, you okay?"

"I'm fine," she said, closing out the concerned-looking woman. "Goodbye. I'll call you. Really. Bye, now."

"Mrs. Bishop."

Melanie closed the door and walked back to her bedroom. "Call Deion at work," she commanded, relieved when she saw Juanita's car slowly leave the cul-de-sac.

"Good morning, MJM Portfolio Management."

"This is Melanie Bishop. May I speak to Rod Burke?"

"Just a moment, please."

At least this time she didn't get the baffled silence from the receptionist.

"Melanie, it's Rod. I heard that you've been calling."

"I have, Rod. Deion isn't home from a trip he left from two weeks ago. I'm worried. He hasn't answered his cell and I'm not sure where exactly he is." She'd been weeping so long, her throat was raw. She cleared it, knowing she sounded like a desperate housewife. "Where is he?"

"Melanie, Deion quit working here two weeks ago."

"What?" Shock and panic and a desperate sense that everything was coming to a close enveloped her. He loved his job and if he quit there, he had much bigger plans.

"Deion walked in one day, said he had an opportunity he couldn't pass up and handed in his resignation. I wasn't happy at all, but I couldn't stop him."

"When was this?"

"Exactly two weeks ago today."

"Rod, do you still hold his license?"

"No, I gave it to him. We severed all ties, and he left. Funny thing, though, I thought he was going to try to undercut me and take his top clients, then I'd have recourse to sue him, but he hasn't touched them."

Melanie knew better than to say Deion wouldn't cheat Rod, but that's how Rod had gotten his start—by avoiding his former firm's client list.

"Nothing at all, Rod?"

"Not a peep. Mel, I wish I could help, but I've got a meeting. I don't know any more than I've told you."

"Sorry to bother you."

"No bother. Bye," he said and hung up.

Melanie listened to the dial tone. All communication between her and Rod was probably over forever.

The tears poured from her as she walked from room to room, opening doors, letting her pain fill each space. Open-mouthed she cried out her sorrow in the nursery that would never know the rhapsody of her children's glee. The guest room that had never experienced the joy of a guest, and the master bedroom that had lost its master and mistress.

Tripping on her slippers, she tumbled down the step in the den and lay there, wishing her pain would end. Why hadn't he just told her face-to-face it was over?

How could he break her heart this way?

A hand touched her shoulder and she jumped.

"Mrs. Bishop, why are you crying?"

"Juanita? You're back."

"Yes, ma'am. I was worried about you. Come on, get up. I was afraid. This is my husband, Jusef."

They helped her off the floor and to the sofa. Juanita dispatched her husband to the kitchen for a towel and glass of water. "What's wrong?"

"He left me and I don't know why. Just served me with divorce papers weeks ago and he's gone."

Juanita rubbed Melanie's back and closed her eyes. "Let me pray for you."

Softly in Spanish she prayed for Melanie as Jusef stood in the doorway and waited. When his wife was done, he brought the water. "May I see the papers? I'm in law school."

"You are? Juanita, I didn't know."

Shame filled Melanie because she'd never gotten to know the woman who cleaned her house and had indulged her and Deion's nonsensical wishes. "I'm so sorry."

"No. I came here to do my job not to talk, talk, talk. I do enough of that at home. I'm helping Jusef through law school and then he will help me through culinary arts school. We will do well together."

There was love in this family, Melanie saw, and respect. She wished she'd been able to have that with Deion.

Melanie finished the water and felt better.

"Jusef, the papers are on the dining room table. They're clear-cut and he even signed them. I'm leaving. I was just walking around thinking about all the dreams that were lost, and I guess I got overwhelmed. This morning I accepted a job in Kentucky."

"Are you sure you won't give him a little more time?" Juanita asked, her own eyes sympathetic.

Melanie wiped her tears and accepted Juanita's hug. "No. I talked to his boss and he said Deion quit his job. I've called everyone and nobody's seen him. Nobody knows anything and if they do, nobody's saying. He doesn't want me to find him. It's time to face reality that he's gone for good."

Jusef returned, reading the papers. "You can take what you want. Do you want to contest this?"

"No. He's being more than generous."

"He may have more assets."

"No, I'm not going to fight over anything. I put some things in the car and I shipped my gardening tools and seasonal clothing yesterday."

Juanita looked around. "You didn't take anything."

"I did. Some papers and other smaller things I wanted. I kept the personal things he gave me, but overall I want to make a fresh start. I have money, so I'll buy whatever I need once I get there. Do you need anything, Juanita?"

"No, ma'am. We are just fine."

"Juanita, we need a bed. Our bed is twenty-five years old and we are only thirty. Why are you saying no?" Jusef said. "You didn't learn anything from church on Sunday."

Melanie smiled for the first time in days. "Jusef, I've got just the bed for you."

The next morning, Melanie felt the tears building, but kept them at bay. She swept up the last of the trash and pulled the garbage can to the curb, waited as the garbage man dumped it, then dragged it back to the garage where she hosed it down. She washed her hands, then walked back down the driveway.

"Mrs. Bishop, you sure you want me to take all of this?"

"Yes, please enjoy everything."

Melanie looked at Juanita's overloaded Chevy Trailblazer. She'd filled the SUV with all the items a new couple would need to start a home. Jusef's brother had brought his big truck and had carted away the bed this morning after Jusef and Juanita had awakened. They'd been kind enough to stay overnight with her.

Melanie stood by Juanita's side, then hugged her fiercely. Jusef came down the driveway and handed her the keys. The house was locked up and she couldn't look back.

"I've paid the utilities and taxes. You're going to come by every two weeks to check on the place and make sure nobody bothers it," Melanie said to Juanita, looking at the ground.

"That's right, Mrs. Bishop, I mean, Melanie."

"Here's my number if you need me. The alarm company has your number. If you want to quit, move, or whatever, please call me."

"I won't quit. You paid me a year's salary in advance. If he comes back, shall I call you?"

"No. Just tell him all the bills have been paid, and he's officially divorced."

Melanie climbed into her car, which had been backed down the driveway by Jusef moments ago. He'd turned the Volvo around and positioned it on the cul-de-sac so she wouldn't have to look at the house as she drove away.

"You are sure?" Juanita asked.

"Stop, Nita," Jusef cajoled. "She is ready."

Melanie took a deep breath, then stuck her left hand out the window, and they grasped it and blessed her. She let go first and drove away, tears blurring her eyes, listening to the recording as she drove, "I'm sorry the number you have reached is not in service or has been temporarily disconnected."

Chapter One

"Rolland, you're doing great."

Rolland Jones didn't doubt for a minute that he was doing better than great. When he'd first arrived at Ryder Rehabilitation and Spinal Center, he couldn't even sit up without help. Now he was in a mad race to the finish on his stationary bike against Horace, his physical therapist.

Horace perspired like crazy as if they'd been riding for hours, when they'd been on for only twenty-five minutes. Rolland couldn't help but laugh at the enthusiastic man who never seemed to have a bad day.

"Okay, big Ro," Horace challenged. "What is a biathalon? Forty-five seconds."

Rolland's legs were longer but he stayed at a moderate

pace as he'd been taught. "A biathalon is a cross-country skiing and shooting event."

"Correct." Horace pumped his arms in the air cheering. He picked up his water bottle and used it as a pretend microphone. "And now for the final two thousand points, and to be crowned the unofficial, unolympic winner of the miniature-size trophy of a chocolate candy bar with peanuts, you must answer this question correctly."

Rolland was already laughing. "Give me the question."

"Sir, don't rush the announcer. Who is the all-time highest scoring male basketball team of the U.S. Olympic Games? Sixty seconds." He started an offbeat drumroll that spun crazily throughout the workout room to the other patients and therapists.

Shelby, a physical therapist who occasionally worked with Horace, stopped by. "You're looking good, Rolland," she said, mischievously.

Rolland had no problem identifying Shelby because of her green eyes and red hair. One of the first things he'd learned with his injury was how to associate people with their eye and hair color.

"Shelby, don't cheat and help him, or when you need chocolate, I'm not going to help you."

Shelby's mouth dropped open in mock hurt. "Are you accusing me of impropriety? I thought Horace and I were friends, right, Rolland?"

"That's right, Shelby. I'm hurt for you."

"Shake your head, Rolland," she told him, and he did.

Horace didn't buy it for one second. "You two are full of hot rocks. Shelby," Horace stood pedaling fast, "if you tell him, you're going to suffer. You know how you get. You're gonna need some chocolate."

Rolland laughed. "Give me a hint, Shelby. Come on, my friend. I know where he keeps the candy stashed."

She pretended to fall asleep, with her hands by her cheek. "I'm so tired. I can't wait to go home and have sweet—"

"The Dream Team!" Rolland shouted just as Horace hopped off the bike and ran after Shelby who sought refuge behind two large male nurses.

They grinned at Horace who was the most senior therapist because of his candidacy for his Ph.D. But he maintained a sense of humor about himself and made everyone laugh by jumping around, never quite reaching Shelby.

Horace went around the room, harassing other patients by doing a couple squats with Harold, and some legs lifts with Lavenia, and some arm curls with Maven, until their therapists shooed him away.

Rolland mopped his brow while Horace guzzled water. "Four miles, man. I swear, I think you're trying to kill me."

"Me?" Horace shook his head. "I've lost fifteen pounds since you got here. My wife thinks I've got another woman. I keep telling her it's you." He chuckled. "She can't believe I'm losing weight because of a dude." Horace tried to look disgusted, but lost his frown to a smile. "You're not even my type."

"And people think *I* have the brain injury," Rolland said, playfully shoving Horace as they headed for the weight room. Everyone applauded as they walked by.

Horace bowed on his way out. "Second show, three o'clock," he called.

"Do you think I was in shape before the accident?" Rolland asked him when Horace caught up in the state-of-the-art weight room. They passed the therapy tables where Rolland remembered spending many a day getting his knee back to working order.

"Yes. You had good muscle tone when you got here two months ago. You spent a month in that hospital in Las Vegas and that was to heal the fractures and for reconstructive surgery of your knee. You had good muscle memory. That told me you'd been athletic."

They passed a mirror and Rolland didn't stop and look at himself as he used to. He'd had work done on his face, too, but he was healed for all intent and purposes.

Most of the people here were in some form or another of reconstruction. Be it physical or mental. Fortunately, he was, physically whole. It was his brain that didn't know who he was.

"Come on and show me what you got," Horace said, adjusting the weights to forty pounds for the chest press.

Rolland sat down, planted his feet and breathed through the first ten reps.

"Good. You got ten more in you?"

Rolland nodded. "With this brain injury, do you ever remember your favorite color?"

"Possibly. Good," Horace praised. "Even if you don't, you develop new taste. It's like, do you like green now? Is that important? Is your wife green? Does that matter?"

Rolland laughed. "You're sick, you know that?"

Horace shrugged. "Yes, sir, I do, and I appreciate my gift. You're meeting someone new today. Melanie Wysh. W-y-s-h. Wysh. It's not the conventional way you'd spell *wish*."

"No?"

"No. That's w-i-s-h. A good sentence would be I wish I was taller than you. You're an average-looking bloke at six-feet tall, and I'm smashing looking at five-foot eight. Want to try ten more reps?"

"Yes." Rolland did eight and struggled through the last two. He was almost done at Ryder and this Melanie would have a lot to say about his next steps in his life.

Horace handed him ten-pound weights. "Are you comfortable with the weights?"

"Yes. Is Melanie already here?" Rolland asked the same questions each time he was introduced to someone new, but Horace never got tired of them.

"Yes, she is."

"Have I seen her before?"

"Occasionally. She's a tiny woman. About five-four. She wears dresses all the time. Brown-skinned. Nice lady."

"Is she black?"

"Yes, she's a black lady."

"Okay." Rolland closed his eyes and tried to picture her, as his brain flipped through the women he'd met at the facility. He still couldn't place her, but the frustration he used to feel from not remembering someone didn't come today. "What else do you know about her? Is her hair short like Purdy's?"

"Nobody's hair is like Purdy's, and you don't want it to be with that permanent hairnet she wears."

Rolland laughed and pumped the weights. "I don't think I've met Melanie. Has she seen me?"

"No. She hasn't seen your crazy-looking self."

Rolland took the ribbing in stride. "I'm a lot better than I was. I don't know what I looked like before, but this isn't bad, right?"

"You are correct there, my friend. Do ten curls, slowly. Melanie arrived two months ago, but she had to go through training on how to do things the Ryder way, and then she took over cases for Barbara Greenspan who went out early on maternity leave."

"The lady with the cats." Rolland chuckled. "I'm glad she's gone."

Horace held his curled arm for a second, then guided it down. "You scared of cats?"

"I don't know, am I? She had like fifteen cat calendars, cat mugs, cat hats and cat chair covers. Her office is enough to scare anybody."

Horace laughed and Rolland kept pumping iron, alternating arms. "She had a cat clock that chased a mouse. Do they screen people before they hire them here?" Rolland put the weights on his leg and watched Horace lie on the floor and laugh. "Get up. You're making me look bad."

"You'll like Melanie," Horace told him. "She's really good. She'll help you return to society with hardly any glitches."

"Not if she has cats, she won't."

"Now listen, in all seriousness."

Rolland stopped moving. This was their code phrase when to listen closely. "You're almost done here. Physically, you've passed every test. The four-mile ride, and then you shook your head when Shelby was talking to you. Coordination, balance, stamina. You did it."

Rolland leaned back and smiled. "Really? Well I'll be—" he frowned. "I'll be what, Horace?"

"A son of a gun."

"That's right. I'll be a son of a gun. Why aren't we celebrating with some of that bad chocolate cake Purdy cooks in the lunch room?"

"You have high-class taste buds, too, but don't say that too loud. I like Purdy's food." Horace looked around as if Purdy had spies. He crouched down in front of Rolland. "The truth is that physically you're healed. You might have a little difficulty with balance, but otherwise you're okay. And you've got your cane, if you need it."

"I don't need it."

"Okay," Horace said, putting his hands out, knowing how Rolland felt about it. "We didn't know Barbara was going out early on maternity leave, or we'd have already started you with someone on the last phase of your treatment."

"I'm not mad about that, Horace."

"I know the cat thing. Melanie is taking you on as a favor to Barbara. You have to get past Melanie Wysh before you can go into the world. You may never remember your old life, but you can start a new one. She's the gatekeeper."

"Melanie has the key, right?" Rolland said slowly.

"That's right. Your memory is getting better every day. You're remembering all the new things you've been taught. I feel as if my child is growing up and going off into the world."

"I'll miss this place."

"You can always come back to visit, but once you're gone you're going to be fine. I promise. Besides, you'll always know where to find me. Let's finish up and get some cake."

Rolland did ten triceps presses and stretched. The other therapists watched him and he realized they'd been charting his progress all along. These people had become his friends to replace the ones he didn't know if he had.

"Horace, I'm going to shower and change. I want to meet Melanie today. Let's get this last phase started."

The door to the gym opened and Horace looked around him. "I guess you're going to get your wish sooner than later. There's Melanie now."

"Dude, I'm sweaty." Rolland threw the towel over his face and mopped himself dry.

"She won't care. She's down-to-earth people, like me. Melanie," Horace called. "You might as well meet your new client. Melanie Wysh, this is my pal, Rolland."

Rolland pulled the towel off his head and shoved it under his arm before extending his hand. "I'm sorry for my current state. I'm Rolland."

Her eyes were the color of rust, her skin warm-looking like honey-baked bread. She'd been smiling as she walked, her hair bouncing in frivolous curls. Then she gasped twice and her hand flew to her cheek.

Her lips lost their smile, and she licked her teeth showing just a hint of pink tongue.

"Is everything all right?"

She nodded in a jerky manner.

Her hand fluttered in mid-air and he took it, knowing it would be as soft as it was. He'd learned people would sometimes react oddly to him and he forgave her.

"I'm Melanie Wysh," she said. "And your name again?" She reclaimed her hand and put it behind her back. Her hair was red. He loved red hair.

"I don't know. Three months ago it became Rolland Jones."

Chapter Two

The colored letters on the side of Rolland's case file seemed to follow her as she walked barefoot through her cottage home. Melanie carried the glass of wine to the living room sectional and sat down, folding her legs beneath her.

Plumping the pillows, she leaned back and felt her back relax, yet the tension in her body remained until she reached for the file that had dominated her mind. She used her fingernail and opened it.

John Doe aka Rolland Jones had been in a car accident in Las Vegas, Nevada, June 16, a little over three months ago.

His injury list was extensive. Broken nose and eye socket. Dislocated jaw. His front six top and bottom teeth had been knocked out. Sustained lacerations to his upper body, arms and hands. The injury list to his knee was gruesome and she winced, and then read, *Traumatic Brain Injury*. He'd been pulled from a car that had burned, but he had been spared injury from the fire.

After lying in a coma for twenty days, he'd been brought to the Ryder Rehabilitation and Spinal Center in Kentucky for complete rehabilitation.

His physical recovery had been nothing short of miraculous, except for the resulting symptoms from TBI. He knew how to write alphabetical letters and words, but he couldn't write numbers anymore. He reversed things, his shoes occasionally, words, which hand to shake with. He had image memories of his past, but not of the past six years. Sometimes things had to be defined for him. He didn't know his name, his age, but he thought he'd been married. He confused right and left and didn't have a mental edit button. Whatever he thought came right out of his mouth. He still suffered with balance problems and he sometimes got lost.

Melanie raked her hands through her new short haircut and stared at the auburn strand that came away between her fingers. Why had she dyed her hair this color?

Because it was different and she'd wanted a fresh new look to go with her new life.

She did a few deep breathing exercises. How could she help Rolland Jones?

She jotted down the standard treatment plan, but given his physical advancement, decided maybe Mr. Jones might like to do some of his therapy outdoors.

He was handsome. Gorgeous, really and she wondered why she hadn't spotted him before. She'd heard his name mentioned several times, but had never known who the women in the break room had been talking about.

She tried to put Rolland to words and realized there weren't enough. He was the mmmph women talked about with a shake of their heads and an open-mouth laugh. He was the reason for the raised eyebrows and the twisted lip at the laundry center. He was the double sigh, neck roll, wrist flick, teeth suck, hip switch, six feet of mocha-mocha, hot, scarred, but still fine black man.

She rubbed her aching heart with her thumb, telling herself love was not in her cards. She was here to help make others whole so they could go into the world and become productive.

Her time had decidedly passed.

Sipping her wine, she closed her eyes and listened to the water and the sounds of the children playing around the man-made lake outside.

It was September, typically hot in Georgia this time of year, but Kentucky boasted moderate temperatures with low humidity, and she was glad she'd chosen this place to relocate.

The vacationing families had left after the holiday, and everyone who had stayed had already gotten acquainted.

She'd been welcomed, and while grateful for the warm reception, Melanie liked that her neighbors respected her desire for privacy. After her initial refusal to be set up with everyone's brothers, they left her dating life alone.

She leaned back on her pillows, the file on her chest, watching the sun fade behind the Appalachian Mountains.

How could she give Rolland Jones reasonable hope that he'd be all right in the world without any help? Most TBI patients had family to aid their recovery in the outside world. Having TBI wasn't easy. It wasn't like he was ever going to wake up and not have the debilitating condition.

His brain would not be restored to its former state, but she could help make his life reasonably comfortable. Her job was to make sure he had the skills, but not to give him false hope. She'd teach him how to live within his limits.

Resting her eyes, Melanie listened to the distant strains of Michael Bublé singing *Me and Mrs. Jones* on the stereo and dozed.

Melanie stood behind her desk, then on the side, then sat in the visitor's chair, then went back behind her desk.

Where was Mr. Jones? He was thirty minutes late.

Walking to the door she peered out and then decided she wasn't going to search for him, but get some other work done. She had other clients to see besides him.

Melanie sat down, then got up to adjust her fan to blow right on her, because her office got too much morning sun. She held her arms out so she wouldn't perspire all over her summer sweater as she reviewed two client charts. Making notes, she reached for her diet soda.

"Soda isn't good for you."

His voice made her feel as if a hundred hands were bathing her with warm oil.

"You're late. I expected you at ten."

He looked at her, then down at the card in his hand. Large hands, capable hands turned the card over and she wondered what else they could do.

She pulled her gaze away.

"Melanie, I'm sorry. I can reschedule." His sincerity made her feel guilty for being so blunt.

"Oh. Okay," she said taken aback. Her husband had never apologized for anything. "Of course not. I'll see you."

"I get times wrong sometimes, but this says eleven o'clock. I can't read numbers anymore. Although that may say ten o'clock. It looks like it says eleven." He walked inside the office and came around her desk, the card extended. "You can see for yourself, I wouldn't lie to you."

The last few months, she'd uncovered so many untruths that Deion had told, she'd stopped believing in anything. She had to remind herself that they weren't the same people.

"I didn't mean to imply that you'd lied, Rolland." She tried to rise just as he leaned down to show her the card.

Their heads connected and the card fell to the floor.

"Ow!"

"Oh," he said, backing up, a smile as big as sunshine on his face.

"Are you okay?" she asked, up and out of her chair in an instant. "*I'm* sorry. Is there a bump? Can you see me? Are you having any trouble?"

"Melanie?" His voice moved boulders in her.

"Yes?"

"My foot hurts."

She looked down and realized she was standing on tiptoe on his toes. "Oh my goodness, I'm going to kill you. No! That's a figure of speech. I'm so sorry. I didn't mean that."

He laughed now, sidestepping his foot from beneath hers. "I think I'd better sit down."

"Of course. Come over here to the couch. I'll get some ice."

"It's just a head butt. You didn't hit me with a Crown Victoria. Now that needed some ice."

Melanie hurried across the hall to the break room and was back in a few seconds with an ice pack.

Rolland had sat on the couch with his head back. A knot the size of a pea had formed on his forehead close to his hairline.

"A Crown Vic hit you? Who drives those these days?" Melanie studied the knot, trying to decide how to apply the pack that was now freezing her fingers.

"Old people. Well, in my case their granddaughter who wanted to sneak out on the town. They're paying for my care and offered a healthy settlement, which I accepted."

"I'm glad you're being taken care of."

He touched her wrist. "You sound like you really mean that."

"Of course I mean it. Everyone here wants the best for you."

"Melanie?"

"Yes," she said, holding the pack by her fingertips.

"I think we might need to cover that with something or when you take it off, you might peel off my new skin."

Mortified, Melanie stepped away. She was standing between his legs. Looking down into his eyes, all she wanted to do was cup his face and ask him where had he been all her life?

She knew the thought was irrational and she'd have a serious talk with herself tonight over sushi. But for right now, she was not going to cause him further harm.

"Rolland, I'm a very capable rehabilitation specialist. I didn't mean to hurt you, but I've clearly started on the wrong foot. I'm going to get a towel, apply this pack and then call someone to check out your head."

"That's not necessary, Melanie. I've had worse injuries playing football."

Melanie hurried to her desk and opened her lunch bag. "So you remember playing football?"

"Yes, when I was a kid. I remember running with the ball and laughing. But not my name, the team and all that. A cloth napkin," he asked, once she wrapped the pack and put it on his head.

"They make me feel special." Melanie tried not to look down at him.

"I feel pretty special for you letting me use it," he said.

"And you should," she tried to joke. "I don't usually do wound treatment. But considering I caused this bit of trouble, I'm obliged to help you."

"Thanks," he said smiling.

"So what do you hope to learn, Rolland?"

"How to cook. Add numbers."

"Like nine plus seven?"

"That's going to take me a few minutes. Write numbers. I recognize it's a number, but I can't write it for anything."

"The alphabet." Melanie listened as he recited the whole thing without stumbling. "Backwards."

"You're kidding."

She smiled, surprised at herself. "Yes, I am. What else can you identify that you want to learn?"

"I want to find out about my old life. Was I married? Did I have a family? Where are they? Did they look for me? I want to learn how to drive. I love cars."

"Well," she said. "Some of those things are on my list, too. Learning how to use numbers so you can dial a phone and cook are very important."

"Do you use lists a lot?" he asked, gazing up at her.

It occurred to Melanie that she didn't have to stand over him and hold the ice pack. "Yes, for everything. It helps you stay on task and helps me track your progress. You don't like lists? Here, hold this."

She guided his hand up to hold the ice pack and went back to her desk and sat. Feeling silly for leaving him on the couch alone, she took her pad and the contract she had every client sign.

"Lists are fine, but you have to keep them in the right, what's the word?"

"Perspective?" she offered.

"Right. Everything has a right perspective. So let's get started. Am I going to learn how to cook first or drive?"

She laughed. "No, but I was thinking, the most important thing for you is to always know your way home, right?"

"I don't know that I'll ever find my home, Melanie."

Her heart pounded. "You—you will, Rolland, and you know, I've found, a home is wherever you make it. But first thing's first. I'm giving you a contract and by tomorrow I want you to read it and sign it. If you don't understand something, just ask me and I'll explain it to you."

"I've got homework already, Melanie Wysh."

"That's right. Now, here's a compass. Let's go get lost and find our way back. I just need to do one thing."

She went behind her desk and changed her pumps to sandals.

Coming back to his side he looked down at her. "You're short."

"Thanks, Rolland, that was honest."

"Was I supposed to lie?"

She saw the confused look on his face. Bless his heart, he really didn't know social rules. "No, you're not supposed to lie, but you're not supposed to say everything you think, either."

He towered above her by more than half a foot.

"What are you thinking?" she asked.

"I get what you're saying. Shelby perspires like a man and some of the guys joke about it in the locker room. I'm not going to tell her."

Melanie laughed. "Good example. Don't ever tell her. Now let's go?"

Rolland stepped outside and Melanie closed her door behind them. She pushed her sunglasses in place before joining Rolland and heading out into the sunny and breezy day.

"I love the color of your hair." He let his palm touch the spikes and smiled down at her.

"Thank you, Rolland. Now, you know north, south, east, west, right?"

He stopped at the intersecting sidewalk and shook his head. "The cafeteria is blue. The dorms are brick red. The gym roof is orange and rehab center is white. The administration offices are beige. If north isn't a color, you have to tell me where it is."

Even though she had on her sunglasses, Melanie had to lean backward to use her hand to shade her eyes because Rolland was so tall. "Okay, this is a compass. North faces the sun. Anywhere in the world. North always faces the sun." She showed him the compass in her hand and looked at his, but they weren't reading the same.

"Hold on a second." She took his and shook it. "Yours is broken."

"You trying to get me lost already?"

"No," she said, banging on the instrument. She stopped hitting it. "Rolland, don't follow my bad example. Hitting something never makes it work."

He laughed. "If you say so. We'll just have to use yours."

"Okay," she said, more softly than she intended. Clearing her throat, she held her compass out and the needle pointed north. "We're facing north. Behind us is south. To our left is west and to our right is east. Okay, let's walk west. Which way is west, Rolland?"

"Right," he said and stepped on her foot.

"No," she yelled too late.

"Oh. Sorry. I didn't mean that. Okay, let's try it again. West is left and we're going left," he sang and walked to his right.

Melanie screamed when he stepped on her foot the second time.

Rolland jumped, and she slammed her hand over her mouth.

Neither of them moved.

Other people around them stopped and Melanie waved them away. She was going to recover.

"You scared me," he said.

"You hurt me."

"I didn't mean to."

"I know, Rolland. I'm sorry for scaring you." She reached out but didn't touch him. "Let's try tomorrow. I've got an idea of how we can get this perfect tomorrow, okay?"

"Okay," he said, not looking at her.

"I'm fine, Rolland, really."

"Don't lie to me, Melanie. If you lie, I can't trust you."

"I'm not lying. I promise."

"Yes, you are. Your toes are bleeding," he said, and walked away.

She saw that they were and wished she could take back the words.

Chapter Three

Rolland sat outside his dorm, sunset streaking the sky in blues and mauve. He looked at the book in his hand to verify the color he was witnessing. Yes, it was mauve. Left of pink and right of rose, it was beautiful and calming. He leaned his head back and let the breeze dust his neck in coolness before he sat back up and looked straight at Melanie Wysh.

"Melanie."

"I owe you an apology, Rolland. May I sit down?"

He moved over on the swing and made room for her. "Do you like to swing?" he asked, pushing it with his foot.

"I do. I haven't in a long time," she told him. "I have something to say."

"Then you have to swing for a few minutes. You'll enjoy it. Put your head back like this."

Rolland pulled Melanie's head back just as a happy breeze floated by.

They sat this way for a few minutes and it gave him time to study Melanie undisturbed. She was a tiny woman, no more than a hundred and fifteen pounds, and if she was five three, he was being generous. Her hair was short, freshly cut with auburn/reddish highlights that looked cute with her eye color.

She was a pretty woman, a classy woman, someone he wished had known him long ago. She had kissable lips like the women on TV, but Melanie was real. She was someone he could see himself coming home to and having dinner with.

"Why did you come see me?" he asked her.

She seemed embarrassed to have been caught relaxing. She straightened her spine and folded her hands. "I came to apologize for lying to you earlier. I did it because I didn't want to hurt your feelings—"

Rolland let her drift off, his mouth pursed. "I didn't cut you off," he said, laughing.

"I know you didn't," she jumped in, hurriedly, then laughed. "I just mean to say that it was easier to say I wasn't hurt so that we could get to the greater goal of you learning which way west is."

He gazed at her out of the corner of his eye. "Okay."

"Do you understand anything I've just said?"

"Yes. So it's better to lie than to tell you you've confused the hell out of me."

Melanie crossed her legs and touched his arm and it felt like fire had been set to his limb. Rolland liked the heat and didn't want it to stop. For the past three months he'd been cut, sewn, stapled, massaged, twisted and rehabilitated by so many people that he thought he was immune to the human touch, until now. He moved his arm closer so she would touch him again.

"I don't want you to lie to me. If I've confused you, then tell me. What I mean to say is that I'm sorry for lying to you. It won't happen again."

She drew her hand back.

"So what happens when you don't want to tell me something?"

"I just won't answer you."

"That's not fair, Melanie. That's the only way I get information."

He could tell she was considering what he'd just said.

"As your therapist I have to keep some things confidential, so I'll just tell you it's confidential and you'll have to respect that."

"That's fair." He opened the book he'd been reading and pointed to the sky. "Melanie, have you ever seen mauve? It's a cool color."

She leaned over to look at his book, and he caught a whiff of her perfume. "Yes, it's cool," she said.

"You have to look at the sky," he told her.

"Oh." She sat back embarrassed.

"You don't have to be embarrassed. I know cool has two meanings."

"You're a mess."

He looked down at his clothes, then at her and she started laughing until her meaning dawned on him. "Oh, you're funny. Mess has two meanings. I can see therapy will be fun with you."

"What do you do when you get upset?" she asked him as they watched people walk the large campus.

"I try to figure out what went wrong," he said, crossing his legs. "I never get angry with people. I get disappointed. I mean, what can anyone do to make me angry? They're trying to help me. If they don't give me cake? Sometimes that's not so bad."

She smiled and his stomach fluttered.

"This is all I know. So I don't get angry. I get frustrated. I want to leave the campus and come back like real people do. I feel like you're all having more fun than I am."

"What kind of fun?"

"Driving."

She laughed. "Driving is important, but I wouldn't say it's fun."

"You have your arm out the window, your sunglasses on. You wave to people, blow your horn. You're going somewhere. It's fun."

"You've seen me driving?"

"Yes, I've seen everyone driving. Even Purdy and she's not a good driver. She's hit everybody's car."

Melanie's mouth fell open. "No way."

"Does that mean am I lying? I'm not. I've seen her. Horace and I have seen her hit cars in the parking lot."

Melanie cracked up and looked around. "Did Horace tell you not to tell people?"

He considered her question for a moment. "Maybe he did."

She patted his arm. "Let's talk about something else. May I ask you something?"

"My life as far as I remember it is an open book."

"Okay," she said, and he liked the way she squeezed her lips together. "Why don't you have a sock on your left foot?"

He stretched his long leg out and flexed his foot.

"Melanie, we were having a hard time earlier with west. I'm not sure if it was me, but let's just say it was. I decided that to spare your foot anymore damage, I wouldn't wear a sock on this foot as long as your toes are healing. No sock will remind me that left is west." He stood up. "Left is west," he said and turned left.

Melanie applauded. "If left is west, which way is south?"

Rolland stopped and closed his eyes. Other patients and their family members walking by on their way to the dorm watched Rolland.

Melanie gave them the sign to be quiet.

"If you're facing north and west is left of north, then south is left of west?" Rolland pivoted to the left and looked at Melanie expectantly.

"Yes! Rolland, that was great." She'd gotten off the swing and hurried over to him. "Which way is east?"

"Left," he said confidently.

And she gritted her teeth and jumped before he could catch her toes.

"We'll work on it," she told him. "You did great."

"Almost perfect. Horace would say I got too cocky trying to impress you."

"Impress me? Why?" Her smile faded a little.

"You're my new therapist and who wouldn't want to impress the person who holds their future in the center of their hands?"

"In the *palm* of my hands."

He took her hand and drew a circle in the center. "Right, and that's a lot of responsibility to place right there. Besides, you're beautiful and when I see you, I get a fluttering feeling in my stomach."

"Oh, Rolland." She drew her hand back and her smile disappeared.

"It's not like when they gave me the medicine that made me throw up, Melanie. Now you look ill."

"No." She reached for him and her hand stopped midair. Then she touched him anyway. "I'm not ill. It's just—well. Do you understand about relationships? Man and woman relationships?"

"I wasn't born yesterday. I didn't forget everything. I see how these women look at me. I'm scared of 'em."

She nearly laughed, but smothered it behind pursed lips. "Right. Why?"

"They whisper when I walk by, but I can still hear. Once I got my new face, well, I was the cat's meow."

Melanie burst out laughing and tried to hide behind her hand. "Who told you that?"

"The optometrist who worked on my eye after my facial bones healed. I had been developing cataracts, so I had Lasik surgery to fix everything."

"No." She looked horrified, but remembered reading this in his file.

"Dr. Hoover said I was the cat's meow."

"Okay, don't you say that again."

"Why?"

"Men don't say that about themselves."

"What do they say?"

"Nothing."

"Women say they're hot, cute, sexy, and men can't say anything?"

Melanie looked lost. The sidewalk lights flickered on and he could fully see her face. "I'm not a guy. I don't know what they say."

"But it's not the cat's—"

"Don't keep saying it." Her hand was on his arm in a strong grip, her lips threatening to smile again.

"Melanie, I get a lot of attention and I've never been attracted to anyone. Not a doctor, nurse, aide, therapist or driver, and I think that covers just about everyone—until I met you. You're very pretty and not just in that you-put-on-makeup way, but I like you. More than Purdy, but not more than Horace."

She looked so serious for a moment and then she burst out laughing. "*Not* more than Horace? Okay, that's fair. You've known him longer. Okay, but this is the deal, Rolland—"

"I like when you say my name. It sounds as if you really mean to get my attention."

"I do. I need for you to hear this. We have to maintain a businesslike relationship."

"Sit down, Melanie."

He sat on the grass while she continued to stand. Her legs were at his eye level and he got a good view of her legs.

"Your legs are smooth."

She quickly sat beside him.

"I understand that you can't like me in a romantic way. We have to maintain a professional distance. But I can't be honest some of the time, Melanie. See, you missed it."

She looked up as a streak faded in the sky. "What did I miss?"

"The fireworks. There's a company that sets them off every Monday even though the big shots at Ryder get angry."

Melanie finally looked at him and she wasn't angry anymore. "Why do they get angry?"

"Because they feel as if it's distracting to those of us with brain injuries, but we disagree. Look behind you."

Melanie turned around and then looked at Rolland. "Everybody is outside."

"It's kind of special. If you watch long enough you can tell what they're practicing for. Fourth of July, New Year's. Sometimes people even have them for weddings."

The words Happy Birthda glittered into the sky and everyone laughed because the *Y* was missing.

"I've never known this to go on," Melanie said, watching for the next fireworks. Suddenly a pink *Y* sizzled in the navy blue sky, and the audience applauded.

"You probably leave on time. Why are you here so late today?"

"Because I wanted to make sure that I talked to you. Now that we've talked, I'm going to head home."

She stood up and people started making catcalls at her until she ducked down onto the ground. "It's a tough crowd," he told her. "This is entertainment, but you get to drive."

Melanie laughed and took out a small notepad. "I'll make a note in your chart that you want to learn how to drive."

"And I want to be your friend."

"Rolland—"

"Melanie, I've been here for over three months and nobody has looked for me. My fingerprints were taken in Vegas where the accident happened and nothing. They were sent across the country and nothing. Horace said I was born to wolves, but that's not true."

"No, it isn't. He shouldn't tell you that."

"He's just kidding. If he didn't get me to laugh, he'd have a crying man on his hands and that wouldn't have been any fun either. You know what, Melanie? I must not have been a nice person. How big of an ass do you have to be for nobody to care for you or even ask about you?"

"Maybe they didn't know where to look," she offered, her gaze on the ground. When she looked at him her eyes seemed to be filled with tears.

"Don't spend any tears on me."

"Okay."

"My prints came back negative. My wallet and brief-case burned in the fire. That's why I'm Rolland Jones. I got this flutter in my stomach for you, but I've had a busted face and knee that hurt and a whole lot of really painful injuries. I need friends. I'll get over this flutter like I've gotten over everything else. Be my friend, Melanie."

"Okay, Rolland. Let's be friends."

He stuck out his hand and she shook it and by damn if his whole body didn't tingle.

Chapter Four

"Melanie, not feeling well?"

She passed two of her colleagues on the way into the building and reached for the door. "I'm fine, thanks."

"All right, then."

She saw the curious glances but ignored them. So what if she was dressed a little differently? She had to make a point.

Walking into her office, she stowed her briefcase under her desk and sat down. She had just a few minutes to get a cup of coffee before Rolland arrived for his session. She'd spent the greater part of the evening thinking of how to discourage any further advancement of his crush, but the truth of the matter was that when she'd shaken his hand last night, something had happened.

It was as if a fizzler had been placed beneath her skin and ignited because she'd spent the rest of the evening massaging her arm to rid it of the stimulation.

How had that happened?

She had to remember he was her patient. Blowing out a disgusted breath, she grabbed her cup and went to the break room where she met more curious stares. Two therapists finished their coffee and walked out and she was left alone with the one woman she liked the least.

"Why are you dressed like you belong on the prairie?"

The department's administrative assistant Cali loved to attract attention and she did it by wearing as little as possible. She walked over to the coffeemaker, stuck her cup in front of Melanie's and brewed a cup of cappuccino.

"Thank you for noticing my pretty dress. I like it, too," Melanie said.

She handed Cali her cup and the younger woman smiled sweetly. "Don't try to use that reverse psychology on me. I'm too smart for that. That's an ugly dress and you know it. If you don't, you do now. And good luck at the patient softball picnic in that awful thing."

The younger woman was almost out the door. "Cali, don't mistake my kindness for weakness. If you value your job, you'll remember your position and you'll remember mine, too."

All pretense was gone, replaced by a look of hate on Cali's face. "You think you can come in here and just replace my best friend. Well, I'm going to do everything I can to make sure you don't last in your position."

"I'm glad I know where you stand."

"Don't get comfortable." With a twist of her blond head, she walked out, her hip bumping the door, making it hit the wall. For all her theatrics, she nearly ran into Rolland who was oblivious to her drama.

"Hey, Cali."

"Oh, hi."

He stuck his head in the break room. "It's ten o'clock and I believe we have a date with a compass."

Melanie emptied her cup into the sink and rinsed it as she took several deep cleansing breaths. "You're right we do."

"You do know it's going to be ninety degrees today." He eyed her dress skeptically.

Melanie sighed, having not taken that into consideration when looking at clothes to completely cover her body. "I can handle it."

"All right. But you look like you belong on that TV show."

"Little House on the Prairie?" she asked, getting her sunglasses out of her desk and heading toward the door.

"No. *What Not to Wear.*"

"That's not funny at all, Rolland."

Rolland laughed aloud as they kept walking through the woods, birds flapping overhead, disturbed at his apparent glee. He'd made another joke about how old-fashioned her dress was.

"I'm sorry, Melanie."

How could she stay mad at him when he looked so

handsome and so contrite at the same time? He was cool in his khaki shorts and blue golf shirt.

"Do you accept my apology?"

She'd folded her arms and had stopped walking, but she smacked his outstretched hand. "Of course I do. I never hold a grudge. Come on. Where are we?"

"I don't know."

"Rolland, you can't say you don't know. Look at your compass."

"Melanie, I don't know where you got these compasses from, possibly the same place you got your dress, but it says south."

Despite herself, she giggled and pretended to punch him in the arm. She pulled the collar away from her throat and wouldn't admit the dress was a bad choice. Or that the lace was scratching her neck so bad she thought she was about to be beheaded. Or that she wished she had worn shorts like Rolland. And that his legs looked good, despite the neatly sewn scars.

It had been her idea to take the trail into the woods, "get lost" and find their way out. They were still on Ryder property, but she wanted him to find his way back to the campus.

"Stop cracking on my dress. I happen to like it. A friend gave it to me."

"You should give it back."

"What's wrong with it?"

"It's not you. You're short, so why buy a short woman a long dress unless you don't know anything about women."

"What do you know about them?"

He stopped in the middle of the path, put his hands on his hips and struck the pose of the Greek God Zeus. "I've made love to beautiful women, Melanie. You're a beautiful woman and whoever gave you that dress wasn't thinking of you as a woman."

Her throat closed and she had to open her mouth and take a deep breath. "How do you believe they were thinking of me?"

"As an object."

A squirrel rustled the leaves and branches behind her and she jumped.

Rolland took her hand and urged her on. "You have a nice figure. Why cover it up?"

"I have a professional job and I have to dress a certain way."

"You're not Cali. You're not making a statement with your clothes, but you will be if you start wearing that to work all the time. It's like a blanket."

"Who are you?" she murmured, then shook her head, hearing herself. "Let me see that compass. The object of the compass is to let it do its job. It will locate the sun. Where is the center? Do you remember?"

"North, northwest."

"Okay, then we want to figure out where we are." She paused and fanned herself. "It's supposed to be fall. Where are the cool temperatures?"

"You do listen to the weather, don't you?"

"Of course."

"Then you know we're having an Indian summer."

She hadn't known that. "Study the compass, Rolland."

He shrugged. "Okay."

There was a bridge ahead that crossed a small creek. "Do you like to cook?"

"Yeah."

"When was the last time you cooked some food?"

"Uh, I don't know. But if I could cook something today, I'd make sirloin steak, grilled asparagus, fresh baked apple pie over a bed of rice and red wine."

"That sounds delicious. Are you sure you'd put the pie over the rice?"

"Yeah, definitely. Do you like asparagus?"

"Sometimes. Do you?"

"I don't know. I've never had them."

"Rolland, where did you get the menu if you've never had the food?"

"TV. When I was recuperating I watched all those chef shows where the head chef would yell at the other chefs."

"That's terrible." She headed across the bridge and liked the sound of the brook beneath.

"You become sadistic when your bones take six weeks to heal. I got crazy for a while—I'd yell, 'burn the chef.' I didn't say I was a nice person, Melanie."

She couldn't stop herself from laughing. "You're right, you didn't. I suppose I can't hold it against you given your state."

He spun around and walked backward and she watched him. "I have another great menu." The delight in his eyes was captivating.

"Okay, tell me."

"I'd make veal amandine."

"What side dishes?"

"Vanilla ice cream, sweet potatoes and corn."

"You're just trying to make me laugh and it's not going to work."

"If you bake the corn with the sweet potatoes, it's really good. Somebody needs to watch more TV."

"I'm sorry. I shouldn't have teased you. I've never had it, Is it really good?"

"I don't know. I'm just messing with you."

"Rolland, you're a mess."

He looked down at his shirt again.

"Not really. Come on. Let's look at these flowers. Do you know what a rose smells like?"

"A rose."

"Okay, smarty-pants, but what does it smell like?"

"A plant."

"You know there's a difference between flowers and plants." She walked him over to a bush and pulled one down. She smelled it and offered it to him.

"I like watching you, Melanie. You look like you're enjoying it."

"Now you try."

He smelled the flower and then took his time working the pink blossom from the branch.

"What does it smell like?"

"Fresh air."

"Think about it. Does it smell sweet or fruity?"

"I can't tell."

"Try again, Rolland. And this time, really focus."

"Should I smell the flower just like you?"

"Yes. Now focus."

He closed his eyes and inhaled. His chest rose and his Adam's apple moved up and down as if he were eating something. Slowly his eyes opened and when their gazes met, there was sunlight in his eyes.

"What does it smell like?"

"It smells sweet."

"Rolland, that was very good."

They walked on and she chose daffodils and hydrangeas, petunias and more roses, until Rolland found a tree and sat down underneath its shade.

"Can you spread out your blanket so we can rest?" He pointed at her dress.

"Okay, I've heard enough about the dress. It will never see the light of day again."

"Good. And I'm getting a headache from smelling all your flowers." He sat down with his back against the trunk. Although he always had a smile on his face, he looked tired, more tired than she'd ever seen him. She wanted to stroke the back of his neck and rub his shoulders, but that wouldn't have been appropriate. That didn't stop her from soothing him.

"I'm sorry. I didn't mean to overload your senses. We can head back." She fanned him with her hand and gauged the distance back to the dorm.

"Melanie?"

"Yes?"

Kneeling beside him, she put her hand on his forehead and saw the marks on her finger from the absent ring. The reminders of her past life. "How about if I call for a ride for you? They can have a golf cart over here in ten minutes."

Rolland held her until she was still. "Besides liking that you're blocking the sun, I would really like to kiss you."

His lips greeted hers in a kiss that defined perfection in its simplicity. There was a knowing about the way his mouth moved over hers, an assuredness in how his head tilted and hers dropped to the side and back to accept his mouth and tongue that made her realize this wouldn't be the last time. That thought brought reality screeching back.

She planted both her hands against his chest and moved herself away.

"Melanie?"

"Wait. I need a minute." All of her senses began to work again and she heard birds caw. Squirrels hustled about their business, and a deer ran past heading east.

Rolland got closer and even though she didn't want to, she had to stop him.

"Rolland, I could lose my job. You can't do that again. I have to think about the ethical implications of kissing you. You're a patient at this center and I could be held responsible for anything that happens to you."

"I kissed you. I'm responsible for my actions."

"But Rolland, I kissed you back. Therefore I'm responsible, too."

Rolland watched Melanie pace in front of him and wasn't sure what to think of her. Her lips had been so soft and…welcoming. Like they'd been happy to feel him.

He'd never known that feeling. And if he had forgotten he was glad he was able to experience it again. Melanie walked off, and then she was back standing over him with a scared expression on her face. That expression he'd known lots of times. And it had never been associated with something that had felt so right. Maybe he *was* wrong and following his natural instinct had crossed some invisible line.

Since he'd been at Ryder he'd never wanted to be wrong. They had lots of rules. Written rules, unspoken rules and social rules that he'd followed as he'd learned them, but this one of not liking her, he was glad to break until now. She looked terribly sad and he didn't want her to be unhappy.

"Are you ready to leave?"

"Rolland, you have to swear you won't tell anyone what happened here."

The thought of telling anyone something so personal had never crossed his mind. But the troubled look on her face confirmed his suspicions. Kissing her wasn't something he could even joke about in the locker room.

But it had felt so right, so perfect that he wished a part of her had enjoyed just the smallest bit of it. "I would never tell anyone."

No, this was all his to enjoy, no matter how sad she looked now.

Melanie kneeled beside him.

"Not even Horace, and I know that's asking a lot because he's your best friend. If you don't think you can do it, I'll quit now and leave. I can find work some-where else."

"No! What's going on here?"

The sun beamed down on him, but he felt as if ice had been sprinkled on his body in shavings like when his temperature had spiked in Vegas.

"Nothing, Rolland. It just can't happen again."

"Why'd you kiss me? Are you attracted to me?"

"No."

"Do you kiss men you're not attracted to? Are you lying to me?"

When she didn't answer, he started to stand and she put her hand on his arm.

"It's a woman's lie," she finally blurted.

"What's that?"

She looked like she wanted to be sick. "It's the truth, but not a truth I want to admit to. It's something that's very complicated."

"Like those ring marks on your finger?"

She covered up her third finger, then caressed it. "Yes."

"Try me out. I'm a good listener."

"I was married and he divorced me. End of story."

"That's it?"

She nodded.

"That's the lamest story I've ever heard. Tell me what happened to your heart, Melanie. What hap-pened to you?"

"My husband divorced me and I'm still not used to it. Even though it's been three months since I've lived here. Every day before I come in to work, I take off my wedding bands. Today is the first day I decided not to wear them at all anymore."

"Seems like you should be celebrating the first day of your new life."

She shook her head, her eyes distant and sad. Rolland wished he could look out over the sea of flowers and see what she saw.

"I loved…him." She rested her chin on her knees.

"Did he buy you this dress?" She turned and looked at him before nodding. "Well, you should have divorced him first."

She had tiny dimples that became holes when she laughed. "Shut up, Rolland. This is serious."

Her smile had fallen, her gaze resting in the bushes of her memories. "You don't understand."

"Don't use my brain injury against me. I understand a lot. A whole lot." He'd heard this statement so often because it had come out his mouth a million times more.

Startled, her knees buckled and she faced him. "Rolland, calm down. I wasn't trying to offend you. It's a nonsensical statement. I'm sorry. I won't say it again."

He wanted her to know how much he understood, but the words were jumbled in his throat. "I understand a lot, Melanie." He wiped sweat from his brow and flicked it into the grass before wiping his hands on his socks.

"What I should have said is that he didn't really know you. There's fire in you. I felt it in your hands the first time you touched me. My arm tingled. I felt it again when we kissed. So if he divorced you, that's his loss."

She still looked doubtful and he knew what the other

therapists had told him to be true. Only time would make him speak faster and not exhaust him. And only time would make Melanie understand her husband hadn't been worthy of her love.

"You don't know him, Rolland. You can't say that."

"I know I lost a lot, Melanie. I don't know what it was, but I did. Look at my hand."

He showed her his hand and there were no ring lines.

"The thing is, I know in my heart there's supposed to be something there. But for nobody to look for me, tells me what kind of man I was."

Her eyes filled with tears, but he'd shed enough for himself. There would be no more for him.

He stood before offering her a hand up. "I think I've had enough sun for today. Do you smell something burning?"

"I smelled it earlier," she said, patting her cheeks dry. "But I thought it was because they were getting ready for the picnic."

"That's right. You okay?" he asked, picking a few stray twigs from her spiky hair.

"I'm fine. Let's go back. It's been a long day."

They started on the path and Rolland saw the swift moving deer. They were running, heading in the direction of the clearing.

Melanie saw them too and pulled her phone from her pocket and dialed the center, but shook her head. "Nobody is picking up. Let's hurry."

Rolland took her hand and they ran, becoming more alarmed the more animals they saw running in the opposite direction.

The closer they got to the end of the path, the stronger and thicker the smoke. "Stay with me, no matter what," she told him.

"Melanie, I'm a big boy. I can take care of myself."

"I know. But we have to account for all of our patients when there's an emergency, and I don't want to lose you again."

They burst through the clearing and stopped, stunned.

Three buildings were on fire and people wandered the grounds in various states of distress.

"We have to help them," Rolland said and began to run.

Chapter Five

The door of the last ambulance closed and it pulled away, leaving all of the remaining patients and staff in the parking lot. Melanie leaned against the front right quarter panel of her gray Volvo speaking to the director of Ryder on her cell phone.

"Scott, right now they're following instructions and taking everyone to various hospitals and the ambulatory patients to Summit Valley Mental Institution because they have the most room, but that's two and a half hours from my house."

"That's an awful commute. How was Rolland during the emergency?"

"He performed well under pressure. He aided the injured by calming them. I just don't believe SVMI is the right place for him. And to turn his care over to someone there may be detrimental and cause him to suffer setbacks."

"How many weeks do you think he needs before he's ready to be released into society?"

"Conservatively, I'd say four, no more than six. He did very well today." She pushed her finger into her ear as a noisy group of patients walked by.

"Melanie, this is a little unconventional, but I have a summer house about an hour from Ryder, and because he's so close to finishing, I'll allow you to complete your work with Rolland there. It's a nice house, with separate facilities that will make you both comfortable. Some therapists used it last year and found it to be a great retreat."

"You mean for us to stay there? Together?"

"That would be the only way. It's a quiet place, and he can get the intensive treatment he needs. That's if you're comfortable. Otherwise we'll have to send him to SVMI. I can make the calls. We'll compensate you, of course, if you decide to go to the house. I know you'll be bringing most of your teaching supplies with you, but the house has a full gym for his exercise regimen. If you need anything else, buy it and expense it back to Ryder."

"That's very generous of you, Scott."

"Rolland is a special guy and we want him to be successful. I also want you to be comfortable."

"No, he doesn't have to go there. That's too much. Scott, it's a generous offer." Her heart raced. Her palms had grown wet and Melanie was sure she was sweating again.

"What's he doing right now?" Scott asked.

Melanie cuffed her hand so no one else could hear. "He's showing Purdy how to back up without hitting the other cars. But he's not driving. He's using her as the car."

Scott laughed heartily even though it was the crack of dawn in Greece where he was vacationing.

"He's a good guy, Melanie. His progress has been phenomenal and he's got the benefits to pay for his treatment. If his condition worsens, we can get him into any facility we need to, so why not give this a try?"

So much was at risk. So much she couldn't say. But how could she say no? All the other patients were being transferred out. She'd essentially be out of a job. "Okay, Scott, I'll do it."

"Now keep it quiet. A lot of others will want to join you, and I don't have insurance to cover all of Ryder at my summer house. Get a pen, I'll give you the address. There's a lockbox on the door with a key and the garage door opener. I'll be returning early, but I can't get back for at least two days."

Melanie got the information and hung up the phone just as the buses arrived to move everyone to various facilities.

"Rolland, come here. I need to speak to you."

"What's going on?" He jogged over, his clothes full of smoke, his disposition still good.

"We're not going with them," she told him, walking back toward the campus and away from the parking lot.

"We're not?"

"No. Scott has arranged for us to go to his summer house in Springfield, Kentucky, about an hour from here. Everyone else is going to various hospitals and facilities. We feel your therapy is at an advanced stage and that you're ready to put your therapy into practical use. Also, if you were to go to Summit, I wouldn't be able to work with you there."

"Who'd be my therapist?"

"We'd find you a new person."

"But that could take weeks," he said, his eyes never leaving hers. "Why wouldn't you go with us?"

"It's too far to commute. A long way. It's, um, two and a half hours away from my home. Do you understand distance? We've never talked about that before."

"No, I don't, but I know what a long way means."

She smiled at him. "Yes, it's a long way from here. Of course if you'd like to stay with the other patients, then we can arrange for you to be there with your friends, and I would completely understand."

"Melanie, why would I want to do that? People come and go every day. The ob—" he sighed, the words had become more difficult to get out as the day had grown longer. "The objective is to get better and move on. Isn't that what I'm supposed to do?"

She nodded as a fireman escorted her to her office in the building undisturbed by the fire. "Ma'am you have two minutes to get your things."

"Thank you."

"Well, then I'm focused on the goal," Rolland told her. "When do we leave?"

"Now. Can you carry this bag?"

"Sure."

Melanie gathered more folders and pushed them into other bags. "Our first stop will be the store. You need new clothes and we'll need food."

He looked down perplexed. "What's wrong with these?"

"Unless you're planning to wear them every day for four weeks, you'll need some more. Your dorm burned down. One of the grills was too close and somehow the fire got out of hand is what I was told."

His big smile lit up her heart and she had a moment of doubt about the whole idea.

"Melanie, we're going to do well together."

"I hope so."

"Confidence, Melanie. You know so. Which way? Can I drive?"

"I don't think so. Back to the parking lot."

Rolland held the door for her, elated. "Melanie we're making progress. That wasn't a 'no.'"

"West, Rolland. Turn west."

She swallowed the pain when he crunched her toes, but she became very aware of every inch of him when he grabbed her by the waist to steady her.

"I'm sorry."

"It's okay."

"Don't give up on me, Melanie Wysh. I will learn west and east, and north and south, and I will learn how to drive."

She nodded. "I know you will. Let's go."

* * *

"Out of all the cars in the whole world, you chose this car, Melanie?"

She tried not to be annoyed with Rolland and was winning. "Yes. What's wrong with it?"

"It's like your dress. It says the wrong thing about you. It says I'm old and—"

He'd turned around finally as they got into the car at the mall.

"What does it say about me? I'm old and what?" she asked, buckling in.

"Arthritic."

Despite every attempt she'd made not to laugh at his comments about her ugly dress, and her sneakers at dinner tonight, she put her foot on the brake and laughed.

"It's a Volvo, you clown. A fine piece of machinery with classic engineering and style, I might add. Not to mention the fact that not everyone can afford one of these babies. This is a fine vehicle, and safe when you have children."

"But you don't have any."

"I know, but I'd planned on it."

"So you bought the car in advance."

"Yes," she said, feeling slightly uncomfortable. "I thought it was a good investment, and you can keep these cars for fifteen years."

Four teenagers rode by in a jeep. The window flaps were gone giving the breeze free reign in their hair. Music by Shakira, and a strong bass beat made their heads move and she wondered when she'd traded her youth for gardening gloves and a Volvo. She liked Shakira, too.

They looked like they were having the perfect Indian summer.

She gripped the handle of her window and rolled it down.

"Yeah, I can see your son wanting to drive this to the high school dance. What do you call this, Melanie?" He gripped his handle and wound.

"Manual window handle," she told him.

Rolland finished and smacked the dashboard. "Sturdy."

He might have TBI, but even he knew that was ancient. "Come on," she said through gritted teeth.

"I'm not driving," he told her, smiling. Always damned smiling.

So unlike Deion.

Sunset had long since bowed to night and clouds buffeted the sky, making everything seem closer together.

Even in the spacious car, Rolland seemed to be in her lap with his strong legs wide on the seat, his hands folded. The dark night made things more personal somehow, as if the whispers of the couples eating dinner on restaurant patios would forever remain locked in those tiny coves.

Melanie followed Scott's directions to the house aware that Rolland was beside her, his head back, his eyes closed.

She was glad for the break in talking. She needed to gather her thoughts when it came to helping him. Today had been long for both of them and the sooner they got settled, the sooner they could get off to a fresh beginning.

The address on Winterbay Cove was a beach house of indeterminate size with a long driveway that curved up to a sizable garage. Melanie stopped the car and used the code on the lockbox to get the house key and garage door opener. When she slid back in the car and closed the door, Rolland woke up.

Startled, she merely stared at him. "Yes," she said.

"Honey, are we home yet?"

"I beg your pardon?"

Rolland touched his temples. Concerned that he might be having some kind of break, she waited to reassure him. "What's my name?"

"Melanie." He scrubbed his hands over his face, shook his head, looking out the windshield. "Give me a minute." A minute passed, then two, then three. "Melanie. Wysh." He looked as if he wanted to say more, then he tried to undo his seat belt. "Are we here?"

"Yes." She took a deep breath as they watched the three doors on the garage rise.

"That's a whole lot of garage for one car," she murmured. Melanie pushed the buttons for the two doors they wouldn't be using and they closed.

"When you have your kids' toys, it gets a lot smaller," Rolland said. They got out and he stretched. Grabbing four bags, he looked at three doors within the garage. "Which door? Where do these go?"

His offhand statement had been so realistic she didn't know what to say. He had to bend down for her to look in the bag. "It's food. Put it in the kitchen. Better yet, why don't I go inside with you and we can find out about the house together?"

"Good, because I'm tired. It's not every day I save lives and manually roll up my window."

"Somebody doesn't ever want to learn how to drive."

"There has to be something in your contract about you holding things over my head."

She tried two doors with the key. One held water boards and the other yard tools. The third door led to the house. "There isn't," she said, feeling the wall for a switch as they walked in.

She found the fixture and turned it, recognizing the faint buzzing as the house alarm. Hurrying, she put in the code as Scott had instructed and she stared in amazement at the lovely home.

This level of opulence and grandeur had been part of her former life. But she hadn't been in a home this nice in nearly a year. She and Deion had stopped entertaining when she'd become consumed with getting pregnant. Her life had revolved around injections and monitoring her body changes, until seeing their friends and going out had fallen to a level of unimportance.

She'd isolated her husband and shut him out each month that he hadn't delivered the perfect sperm, and now she stood staring at this wonderful home with its rich red kitchen wall, and she wished she could turn back the clock.

"What are you sorry for? You didn't even do anything. I think you're tired," Rolland informed her, yawning as he walked by.

Taken aback, Melanie slid the bags on the table and put her keys on the marble countertop.

"What?" she said.

"You said, 'I'm sorry' as if you had done something."

Rolland passed her again as he went back into the garage.

Melanie softly patted her lips. She hadn't even realized she said it. She wasn't at home within the safety of her own private world. She needed to watch her mouth. "Let me help you," she said, walking into the garage.

"I'm all done. When did you get your clothes? After we ate?"

She nodded. "You dozed off so I dashed into my house and packed a few things. I was out in ten minutes."

"I've never met a woman who moves as fast as you. I wanted to see where you lived."

"Darn," she said, glad that she'd made the decision to stop at her house last. "Let's get you settled in and then I'll put away the food."

"Which button puts the door down for the car?"

"I'll take care of that."

Rolland gave her a look of disbelief. "Melanie, I think we need to get something straight right from the beginning."

Moving bags to the counter, he pulled out a chair for her and one for himself. She sat down and he sat opposite her.

"At Ryder, though we're patients, we are also men and women. We're people who are monitored because we live there and do therapy, but we're also given respect and privacy because we're adults. I don't expect any different here."

"What are you expecting me to do? You're in my charge, Rolland."

"But I'm a man, too."

One of the first things she'd noticed, besides the fresh scars was his muscle tone. She'd always been attracted to men who worked out and were fit, and Rolland more than fit that bill. Right now his hands were inches from her leg and she wanted to stretch out her tired feet and ask for a massage. She knew it would take the strength of an Amazon to resist Rolland, but she'd do it. She'd survived harder temptations. Like the urge to curl up and die when her marriage ended.

"I know you're a man, Rolland. I respect you."

"Then why won't you tell me how to close the door?"

"Oh! Oh." She rubbed the back of her neck, seeing immediately that her desire to control everything was pushing against his desire to function normally. Rolland was different from any other TBI patient she'd ever worked with. He was very highly functional. His reports had said that, but now that she was seeing that for herself, she'd have to modify her treatment plan—and her approach to him as a man.

"Rolland, I apologize. You should know where the button is. Once we finish our talk, I'll show you."

He was encouraged by her agreement. "Thanks. Now, I'll give you your respect and privacy, too, Melanie. I realize you're a healthy woman who has her needs and I would never violate that privacy."

She knew her eyes were widening because she could feel herself blinking faster. This was seventh grade all over again, as embarrassing as sex education class.

"Oh, of course not. I would never intrude upon your private space without knocking and waiting for you to answer. Better yet, I'll wait for you in the common areas of the house. In the living room or here in the kitchen. I won't ever come to your room, Rolland. Oh, my goodness."

"Melanie, I didn't mean to embarrass you."

She touched her face. "I'm not embarrassed." She threw her hands up. "Let's change the subject." She thought it prudent to close her mouth, too. Her lips flattened together.

"No, let's talk about it. Your face is red and you haven't even been running. It's just sex. We talk about it in therapy all the time."

"But not with me." Her face was burning.

"I know, but you can't deny there's a sexual attraction between us." No, she couldn't deny it because that's all she'd been thinking about since he'd become her patient. Since her talk with Scott, and the three-hours drive to this house. All she'd been thinking about was how she'd control herself.

"We can't explore that attraction, Rolland. Scott's entrusted his home to us to complete your therapy and that's what I intend to do. We have to mind our Ps and Qs."

He looked under the table and frowned.

"What are you doing?" she asked, jumping up and pulling groceries from the bags.

"I thought maybe Ps and Qs were like toes."

Melanie realized her mistake. It had been a long time since she'd worked with someone so literal-minded. "No, it's a phrase that means we have to be on our best behavior. Tomorrow we start four weeks of intense therapy that will prepare you for the world. After that you'll go off and start your life all over again, and what happens in the next four weeks will shape the rest of your life. I don't want to mess that up."

"Then you should start thinking positive. I want to make a deal. For every number I learn, you give me a driving lesson."

"Rolland, there are a lot of numbers to learn."

"Then we have a lot of driving to learn. You want me to be safe, don't you?"

She finally nodded. "Okay. Deal."

"Good night, Melanie."

"Okay, good night."

He stood there for a moment.

With her patience wearing thin she turned and looked at him. "What is it now?"

"Can you tell me where the bedroom is?"

"Right, of course. Let's find that together."

Rolland grabbed the bags containing his new clothes

and pulled the suitcase Melanie had packed at her house behind him.

Melanie tucked her pillow under her arm and pulled the handles on her bags, walking through the great room. Overstuffed couches of cream and gold were covered with multicolored and multishaped pillows. All pointed to an ornate fireplace that looked cozy enough for reading or games or even something she'd always thought too corny to try: roasting marshmallows.

"That looks like a sunroom," she said, jutting her chin toward a room off the great room with bay windows, blanketed in darkness.

"Would be perfect for breakfast," Rolland threw out as he lifted her suitcase and carried it. "I don't like the way it sounds on the wood," he said, for the first time looking irritated.

Melanie chastised herself for not being more sensitive. Rolland wasn't the average man who'd just had a long day. They'd been involved in a harrowing experience and now at the end of the day she was expecting him to have regular reactions. She was expecting too much of him. He was tired. She needed to be more sensitive, instead of thinking of herself so much. She was here for him and because of him and she had to remember that.

"We'll start at noon tomorrow."

"Don't spoil me," he said, yawning as they climbed the staircase that looked like they should have been in a classic movie with characters in period costumes.

They walked up the staircase and down a hallway

with green textured wallpaper. "I believe Scott said this was a boy's bedroom."

She pushed the first door open and it was painted pink and white for a little girl. Her breath caught and Melanie backed into Rolland. "I'm sorry, I'm confused. We should be on the other side."

"It's no bother. I can go over there myself, Melanie." he laughed. "Good night."

"I don't mind."

Rolland trailed Melanie as she entered the next room and saw the large four-poster bed, the flat screen TV, the state-of-the-art music system hidden in the cabinet and dresser drawers tucked into the Jack and Jill closets.

"This is the master suite."

Rolland put his bags on the settee and deposited his watch and the contents of his pockets into a beautiful crystal bowl on the dresser.

"Oh, no. Rolland, I don't think that bowl is for knickknacks. It looks like an antique," Melanie said, rushing over.

Rolland was already on the bed and had lain down. He pulled his shirt from the waist of his pants and was scratching his flat abs. Otherwise, he didn't say a word.

Melanie hurried over and then clamped her mouth shut. The inside lip of the bowl said "I eat money."

He hadn't bothered to undress or anything, but lay stretched out on his back, his head tossed to the side, fast asleep.

Melanie searched the closet for an extra blanket.

Finding one, she covered him and tiptoed out the room. As soon as she was in the hallway, she was assaulted by all the emotions she'd been holding back. How was she going to do this? He was too much…man for her. His lips against hers had reminded her of what it felt like to be desired and attractive. His honesty about her dress had hurt, but it had reminded her of what it felt like to be a woman that men noticed. His hands so close to her leg tonight had reminded her of how long it had been since she'd been comforted or her body pleased.

Shaking off the thoughts, she grabbed her bags and found the other master suite and started unpacking. The first thing she did was take off the dress and throw it away. She'd worn it for the wrong reason and it had taught her a lesson. She was a woman and Rolland noticed no matter what she wore.

She didn't need to look like someone on a prairie to divert attention away from her sexuality, but if she were businesslike and organized, they'd stay on track.

Melanie showered and worked for three hours revising her lists and notes. Her eyes grew weary as even the late-night bugs outside packed it in and went to bed, leaving her in silence. Melanie finally gave up around 3 a.m. and fell asleep with a plan in place that a neutron bomb couldn't shake.

Chapter Six

Waking up in the large house was far different than waking up in the dorms at Ryder. Here, there wasn't anyone to talk to. There wasn't any food prepared, and Rolland didn't have to be anywhere in particular at any particular time. The thought put a smile on his face.

He showered and dressed and was downstairs by seven-thirty. Melanie was nowhere to be found. Rolland helped himself to an all-meat sandwich and sat down with a glass of juice and ate. Finishing, he washed his dishes and wiped down the table and his seat, then picked up a pack of green Post-it notes off the counter and started walking through the house. As he passed each wall he put a note to let himself know he'd been there before. Walking down a long hallway off the great room, he found the gym. Turning on the lights, he smiled. There was a weight machine, bench press, tread-mill, bike and rowing machine, Horace's favorite. Free weights were in the corner.

Rolland went in and started his routine and was forty-five minutes into a full-body workout when the door smacked the wall and Melanie walked in. "You can't disappear on me like that." She looked terrified.

"I left you notes."

She squinted at him. "They're on every wall!"

Rolland smiled. "I let you know where I was. You can't be mad at me for that. I didn't go outside. I didn't set off the alarm. And you found me. Did you sleep well?"

He hated seeing that tortured look on her face because Melanie looked like she wanted to cry. Her terry-cloth robe was hiked up and tied in a crooked knot on the side of her stomach. She had one blue sock on and one in her hand as if she'd just remembered he was here and had taken off looking for him. He was glad he hadn't set off the alarm.

He did the last two arm curls and set the ten-pound weights on the floor. "Want to spot me while I do triceps?"

"No! We have serious work to do."

"Exercising is part of my physical therapy. Didn't you know that? I have to do it every day."

She rolled her eyes and a big sigh blew out of her. "Every day?"

"Yes. Horace said I was fit before the accident, but I'm even more fit now. Maybe when I find my family they'll be able to tell me what kind of man I was. I think I was probably not a bodybuilder, but a guy who worked out three or four times a week."

She looked stunned at his assessment of himself and his former life.

Her hair looked like it was screaming and she ran her hand over it. "You were probably a really good man, Rolland. Don't worry about that. Did you eat?"

"I had an all-meat sandwich and juice."

She looked skeptical. "I know you wouldn't have done that at Ryder."

"No, because Purdy isn't here to make me eggs. I'm not supposed to touch the stove. You left a note on it— 'Rolland, don't touch the stove.' I'm not a child, Melanie. That's why I made a man's sandwich. You shouldn't get on me about the little things." He gave her a big grin and sat down on the bench press. Using his shirt, he mopped his face. "When we go to the store again, I need to buy more towels."

"You're right and I'm not angry, Rolland," she said, looking exactly that. "I just can't believe I overslept. It's after nine. I'm usually up before seven and at my desk by eight. I left the note on the stove because I didn't want you to get hurt. I don't know what you remember about cooking and what you don't."

"Okay. But first, you should just put your running clothes on, so we can go before it gets too hot."

An odd expression crossed her face. "This treadmill isn't any good?"

"Just look at the cord."

Melanie went to the back of the machine and made cooing noises. "Their dog must have chewed it. Great. Okay. I'll change. You run?" She looked at him oddly. "I didn't know that."

"You can't know everything about everybody." He rubbed his hands up his wet shirt. "I'm changing to a dry shirt. I'll meet you in the big room in ten minutes, okay?" Rolland pulled off his top and Melanie saw the scars from the accident. He was imperfect and perfect all at the same time.

"Yes, meet me in the great room. Yes, that's perfect."

"Wait! Rolland. Wait up!" Rolland turned around and jogged in place as Melanie flailed her arms and legs to catch up. He didn't want to laugh at her because it wasn't polite.

"You're a terrible runner. Your form is awful."

Melanie gasped for air and plopped down on the sandy beach of the man-made lake. Boaters motored by in the languid green water, while sunbathers rested on the sundecks. "Thank you for that positive feedback."

"You're all over the place. Your arms are flinging, and your feet. I'm surprised you fell only two times."

She looked at him expressionless.

"What does that face mean?" he asked, blocking the sun. She looked like she needed the break.

"It means that I want to say something, but it's not nice, so I'm keeping a cool exterior."

"Okay." He nodded, understanding. "Purdy has that same face when we take our creamed corn back."

Melanie shielded her eyes, looking up at him. "You can't return food in the cafeteria."

Rolland started laughing. "I never knew that. Horace and I do it all the time." He offered her a hand up. "Come on, we have a mile to go. This time keep your arms close to your body and your stride like this." He demonstrated the running technique.

Rolland wasn't sure when the last time Melanie had gone running was, but she was dressed like she hadn't been to the gym in years. Her shorts were almost to her knees and her top was like a basketball jersey he'd seen on TV when they'd shown highlights from the eighties. Long and shapeless, with a white T-shirt beneath it.

"Rolland, I can't. I'm not a natural athlete. I mean, I'm in shape, sort of, but—"

"Melanie, is this the way a patient should hear their therapist talk?"

Her head fell forward, a droplet of sweat coming to the end of her nose. "No, but I wouldn't push you until your body was screaming for mercy. I'm a merciful therapist. You should remember that. So what's it going to be?"

"Let's walk," he said.

"Good choice."

"Fast," he told her and she groaned, but didn't complain again.

The house came into view twenty minutes later and Melanie hit his arm and pointed. "The motherland."

"Melanie, how old are you?"

She shielded her eyes again. "Uh, why?"

"You know a lot about me and I don't know anything about you."

"Well, I guess that's fair. I'm thirty—"

"One," they said together.

"How'd you know?" she asked.

"A lucky guess. O-n-e. One." Rolland felt proud of the woman he felt he knew, but didn't. She was short, really short, even though she had on sneakers and liked to jump up and down.

"You look thirty-one."

"Rolland, that's mean!"

"Really," he said, snatching his arm away as she tried to pinch him.

"Yes," she said.

"Well, really thirty-three."

Melanie chased him and Rolland ran away from the woman who was suddenly very quick.

"Well, how old should I say you look?"

"You never go up," she said, putting her hands on her hips.

He stood six feet away. "So you look about sixteen?"

"No, twenty-five is good. Even if the woman has gray hair and is walking with a cane. Got it?"

"So you can lie about this?"

"Yes. A woman can lie about age. Come on. I have to take another shower."

"Yeah, cause your deodorant stopped working an hour ago."

"Rolland!" She charged after him and he faked her

out twice before she caught him and pretended to wring his neck.

"I give up, Melanie. Your knees are younger than mine."

"By approximately a year."

"How do you know?"

She started walking. "I read your chart."

"That thing is like a government folder. It has everything. Doesn't it?"

"You'd think so. Three plus four. Can you add that?"

"If I had three cars and then I bought four more." He held up one hand and she held up her hand with four fingers raised.

"Seven cars. I'd have three convertibles, one SUV, a Mercedes and a school bus—"

Melanie started laughing. "A school bus?"

"Yeah, I can't just let anybody ride in my convertible. It's made for only two."

"I get the feeling there's a joke coming."

"No jokes, Mel. Some of the people at Ryder need a school bus to get them around, so I'd have a school bus."

"Okay, what else?"

"Uh, I haven't decided on the last one."

"Not a Volvo?"

"Not with those windows," he smiled.

"Can you spell numbers, Rolland? Three?"

"T-h-r-e-e."

"Excellent. You're much farther ahead than most TBI patients."

"I've heard that," he said walking at a leisurely pace, his hands behind his back. "But you never stop learning at Ryder. Everything is a learning experience. Melanie, do you have an accent?"

She smiled and shook her head. "No, I don't, but nobody thinks they do. I grew up in Macon, Georgia, and I went to Georgia State. I married, divorced, and now I'm here with you, and you're on your way back into the world. Have you ever seen a map, Rolland?"

"No. What's a map for?"

"Well, a map can tell you a lot of things. First, maps show you every place in the world, but other maps are more specific. They show you cities, roads, towns and streets."

He shrugged, feeling confused. "Why are we talking about maps when we were talking about you?"

She blinked slowly. "I thought we were moving on to another topic."

"Why would you think that we were talking about you and then maps?" He laughed. "That's a funny..." he thought for a moment, "What's the word when you slide into another topic?"

"Segue?"

He nodded. "Exactly."

She was embarrassed that he wasn't easily distracted and had caught her attempt to avoid the discussion of her life. There was a lot about Rolland she had to rethink. "I'm done stretching. I need a shower and a yogurt, and then we'll get started on your lessons for the day."

"You don't want to stretch your hamstrings? They're going to hurt tomorrow."

"No. I've worked out before. I'll be fine."

"Do you have brothers and sisters?" he asked, stretching muscles that were clearly defined and well-developed. She sighed.

"I do have two sisters and a brother." Melanie looked at her watch. "We really are starting at noon today." The back of the house faced the lake, with a wide deck and grill. "What a gorgeous home. The great room in thirty minutes?"

"Okay," he said, "but I'm going to stretch my hamstrings after my quadriceps. Do you have a mother and father?"

"No, they're deceased and I think that's enough talk about me." She patted his back. "Don't you worry about me. I'm here to help you. Now let's get a move on. We're going to be working late tonight because we got a late start."

Rolland looked at all three easel boards and wasn't sure what he was looking at. "Melanie?"

"Yes, Rolland, I'll be right down. Go ahead and get comfortable on the couch."

He sat down and she hurried down the stairs in jeans, a long-sleeve shirt and a scarf around her neck.

"What is all this?" he asked.

"All the things I think you'll need to know before entering the world." He hated that she looked so happy. He felt his head starting to hurt and he pressed his fingers into his temple and his jaw.

"Tell me what you're feeling," she said.

"Like I want to go back outside where there's more air. Like I want to tell you you look hot."

"Rolland, that's an inappropriate comment. We need to set some ground rules about boundaries. I'm your therapist."

"I know. It's burning up outside and you have a scarf on in the house. Aren't you hot?"

"Oh." She covered her mouth, then her eyes, then her mouth again before putting her hand into her lap. She was quiet for a minute. "My mistake." She put her finger through the knot of the scarf and pulled it off. "Better?"

"I don't understand," he said. "You're angry because I said you look hot. What did I do wrong?"

Melanie sat on the settee and rubbed her spiked hair. "Rolland, some phrases have double meanings. 'You look hot' means you look like you're overheated, or you look really sexy. This is all my fault. I put the scarf on thinking it would give me a professional appearance. Instead I looked hot. That wasn't what I was going for."

"Do you want me to lie and say you look sexy?" he said in a low, confidential voice.

Melanie started laughing. "No, but thank you. That's very kind. Let's just move on and find out why your head started hurting when you saw these easels."

"It looks like we're not going to have fun. Horace made learning fun, like I wasn't learning at all. I never saw a piece of paper. But you have Post-it notes everywhere. This whole sheet of paper is a Post-it note."

Melanie looked embarrassed. "What would you suggest?"

"Keep the little notes and put the big notes away."

"But I need those."

He shook his head. "No, you don't. You can dance with those things. They're so big."

He got up and started swinging an easel around. "Look, Melanie. It's tall enough to be my girlfriend. Come on. Let's put this in the car—" he stopped to think.

"Where do we park cars at home?" she said softly. "The door went up."

"We pulled the car in with the roll-up windows." He accepted her smile. "What is it, Melanie?"

"Is it a bedroom?"

He shook his head. "No, you sleep and dream in your bedroom. You make love in your bedroom."

She blushed.

"Mel, your face is so red."

She giggled. "You say whatever you think, don't you? Don't answer that. What about the kitchen? Can we park in there?"

"No, Purdy would kill us, plus we prepare food in the kitchen." He put down the easel and took the Post-it note and the pen she offered. "Maybe in Syracuse, where Alma from Syracuse is from, you can park your car in the kitchen. But in," he looked in her eyes, "Kentucky, we park our cars in the—" he sat next to her and wrote letters.

"Very good, Rolland, keep going."

He opened his eyes and stared at the letters. "Carport?"

Her smile seemed stuck in place. "Excellent. They're also called garages."

"Garage! That's what I was going for. Carport. Where'd that come from?"

She shrugged. "I don't know. But that's another name for garage depending on your geographical location. You're Southern, is my guess."

"Southern." He squinted. "I watched a lot of Southern movies in rehab."

"What did you learn?"

"Southern men are gentlemen. We open doors, say 'ma'am' and 'sir.' We carry lots of cash, wear big hats, have big jobs, big belt buckles, big boots, big cars, lots of women and have big—"

"Whoa!" She laughed, touching his arm. "Hold on. What kind of movies were you watching?"

"During the day we watched regular TV, but at night the orderlies brought in adult TV. They said we needed to learn how to become men again."

"How terrible of them. Where was this?"

"Vegas. One of the patient's father's was a pastor and when he found out, the learning ended." Rolland sighed. "They got fired, but we had a good time while it lasted."

"I'll bet you did."

"Your face is red again."

"Be quiet." He knew he was working her nerves. They sat in silence for a few minutes. "Rolland, if these easels give you sensory overload, we don't have to work with them. Let's work with our compasses and then I think you should learn how to cook. But before all of that, I have a contract I have all of my patients sign so that we agree on how we're going to work together, and we each give one hundred percent to the effort of you getting better. I noticed you didn't sign it before."

"Then I don't need to. I want to find out about my former life. Why nobody looked for me and who I was. I don't need a piece of paper to tell me that."

"Rolland, I have everyone sign one."

"Then I want a contract that says once I learn your list of things, you'll teach me how to drive, because I've read your list and that's not on there, and if it isn't, then I'm not signing."

"It's not imperative you learn how to drive. We don't even know if that's a realistic possibility."

"I wasn't supposed to live, Melanie. I heard the ambulance driver and the doctors at the hospital. I had a less-than-thirty-percent chance of survival, but I made it and I can speak in complete sentences. Some of my brain is missing, but I'm still here. Take a chance on me. What's the risk?"

She stood up straight as if she was thinking about his counteroffer. "I'll accept your offer, Rolland."

"Let's get started, Mel."

He loved her smile, but he didn't bother to tell her.

Chapter Seven

They practiced writing numbers until Melanie's fingers hurt, but when she took the tracing paper away everything left Rolland's head and he couldn't remember how to do them. But Rolland didn't give up and Melanie was proud. She documented his progress as she watched the rice cook, and then pulled the baked tilapia from the oven. It was perfect.

"Rolland, it's dinnertime."

He was still in the great room with the tracing book. "In a minute."

Melanie shook her head and walked in, putting both her hands gently on his arms. "It's late and you missed the sunset. It's dinnertime. The workday is over. You're not going to get everything in the first day or the first hour."

"I got the number one," he said with a big grin.

His smile disarmed her and made her slow down and look at the long perfect ones he'd written. "Yes, you did. Now can we eat? The asparagus has no nutritional value anymore."

"Toss them. They're nasty anyway."

She laughed. "I'm not. Come on. I've already lost twenty pounds from today's run marathon."

"How are your legs?" Rolland followed her as she duck-walked back to the kitchen. "Your hams hurt, don't they?"

"I'm not talking to you about my legs."

"They feel like you got karate kicked, don't they? We'll take it easy tomorrow. You should consider a new workout outfit, too."

"You're not back on that, are you?"

"You were overdressed and all the flinging around. You need gear that takes the sweat away from your skin. Your muscles won't tire so easily."

Embarrassed, Melanie sat at the marble counter and passed him his plate. She knew all of that and to have a man with a brain injury tell her was just humbling. She'd been overdressed so he wouldn't look at her body, but she'd caused herself a great deal of discomfort. She eased up on the barstool and hid her wince.

"This sweet tea is so good," he said, swallowing a glassful in seconds. "Purdy makes hers and you're sure you're going to have—" he stopped to think about the next word. "What's that disease?"

"Diabetes?"

"Yeah, just like her. She's so funny. She takes her shot and then eats cake. That's scary."

They both chuckled. "I'm going to have a long talk with Purdy the next time I see her," Melanie said. "And there's nothing wrong with my workout clothes. I used to play basketball and that was my uniform."

"Cool. How long ago did you play?"

Melanie shrugged. "Maybe ten years ago."

"And you still have those clothes? You're a woman! Go shopping. That is what Horace says his wife does as her full-time job. Except I thought she was a housewife."

Melanie enjoyed this light side of Rolland. "Excuse you, mister. I shop. But gym clothes weren't ever a priority. I loved to garden and paint the house, and take care of things."

"But you didn't take care of you it sounds like." He had an uncanny ability to cut to the heart of the matter.

She picked up a stalk of asparagus and bit off the head. "How can you say that? We lived in a nice place and it was well-kept. We had a pond in back."

"Who had a pond in back? You or him?"

"*We* did."

"Be honest. It's only me, you and God here. Who wanted the pond. God has the ocean by Florida and New York."

An unexpected giggle burst out of Melanie and she leaned on Rolland. "I'm going to help you with geography as soon as we learn some numbers."

"Mel, don't change the subject. Who wanted the pond?"

"I did, Rolland. They're peaceful. And I thought…
he'd grow to like it. I had live fish in it. I'd chosen these
lovely his-and-her blue-and-beige lawn chairs that were
shaded by this oak tree, and I'd sit under there and watch
the birds come by, and it was absolutely magical. Blue
jays and cardinals—"

Melanie got up and put her dish in the sink, rinsed
it, and then put it in the dishwasher. Talking about her
former life wouldn't bring it back. She was sorry she'd
started down memory lane. Sorry that she'd shared
something so personal. Something that brought tears to
her eyes. Rolland was watching her, she could feel him
and if he only knew…she turned the sprayer on and
rinsed the sink and accidentally got herself a little wet.

"Oh. Look at the mess I've made." He handed her a
towel and she discreetly dabbed her eyes.

"Are you finished? I haven't even eaten."

She looked at his plate and he was right. They'd been
talking so much, he'd barely started. "Okay, less talking
and more eating."

"You have something against eating at the table?" he
asked.

She looked into the dining room that was cast in
darkness. The room was just too formal and reminded her
of her dining room at home. She'd been big on setting
places for her and her husband with matching table mats,
centerpieces and China. She'd loved dinnertime.

"No, I love the dining room, but—"

"Come on, then. If you love something you should
do it all the time."

Rolland didn't know what he was saying. There were things she loved that she could do all the time with a handsome man like him. She realized the direction of her inappropriate thoughts and corrected them. He grabbed her cup and his plate and went into the dining room.

"Rolland, why don't we finish in here for tonight and eat in there tomorrow?"

"Mel, look at that light."

"It's not on."

"I know. But I bet when it comes on, it's going to be nice. Wait, let me put this down." He set his plate on the table along with her glass and then stood back. She finally went in the dining room and stood beside him.

"Rolland, why are we doing this? We were perfectly happy in the kitchen."

"No, we weren't. You like dining rooms and I've never been in one. So, it's like a special day. Okay, this is my special voice." He spoke through his fist. "Mel?"

Nobody had called her Mel since she'd been a kid. Rolland shook something loose in her and made her want to play. Unable to hide her smile, she looked at him. "Yes?"

"You have to have your special voice on." He lifted her fist to her mouth. "Talk like this."

"Okay," she said, unable to stifle her giggle. She lowered her chin and dropped her voice. "What now?"

"This is to mark a big occasion. Two friends who are about to eat in a stranger's dining room are marking this occasion with a song." He looked at her. "Sing something," he whispered.

She shook her head. "I sound terrible."

"Just say la la la la."

Rolland turned around and started again. "Two special friends are marking this occasion with a song—"

"La la la la," she sang in her special voice.

"And dancing from west to east." He stepped left to right. "And then the light ceremony from our singer, Ms. Melanie Wysh!"

Melanie flipped on the lights and Rolland was still dancing from west to east.

"Rolland, you're doing it! You know west and east!"

Melanie jumped up and down and patted him on the back. "That's awesome."

"I've been practicing." He pulled out the chairs and they both sat down.

"When?"

He had a big smile and his normal voice and she could tell he'd been wanting to surprise her. "When you were running up and down the stairs earlier today."

Melanie knew all too well how people with brain injuries processed information. He'd taken advantage of her moments of absence to focus on his tasks. Rolland was doing very well. She owed him a driving lesson...

"Rolland, when you get into a car, you must always wear your seat belt. You must adjust the seat and your mirrors before you start the car."

"Thanks, Mel."

He started on his fish and she didn't want to disturb him now that he was finally eating his dinner. "How many people live in this house?" he asked.

"I think Scott and his wife have three kids."

He studied his hands, squinting. "Five people for this big house. More people should live here.

"I think I have kids, Mel. I probably have eight," he continued.

She shrugged. "Maybe, but maybe not. That's a lot. You'd have to have a really good job."

"Oh, I have a good job."

She leaned on her hand. "What do you do?"

"I'm thinking of a couple things," he said seriously. "I've been thinking about this a lot. First I thought dancer, but there's not a lot of black guys with dancing jobs."

"You're kidding, right?" She chuckled.

"Yes." He ate a forkful of rice. "Really, I think grass cutter. I like being outside. I like grass. I like green grass. Grass cutter isn't a bad job, right?"

She shook her head no. "Not bad at all."

"Did you see the guys today? We were running by and they were standing on the back of their grass cutters and they were laughing. They looked so happy. That's why I think I'm a grass cutter in my old life. I was happy, Mel. But, well… Can you make a lot of money as a grass cutter?"

She tried to stifle her chuckles, but couldn't. "First, you have to stop saying grass cutter. It's called a land-scaping architect or landscaper."

"So there *is* a job for a grass cutter with a nice name, too." He held up his hand for a high five. "I'm on my way back!"

"But the downside is that in the off-season, you

hardly make any money. Besides, look at your hands. If you worked outside, your hands would be hard and you would have calluses. There's a lot more to being a landscaper than riding the back of a lawnmower. You plant bushes, you pull them. You know a lot about flowers and which are good for cold and warm weather. Which ones need lots of water and which are good in dry conditions. It can be a lucrative occupation."

She had his palm in her hand and ran her finger across his inner knuckles. "Do you feel that?"

"Kind of tickles."

"You wouldn't be able to feel that if you were a land-scaper. Is there any other job you like?" she asked, letting go of his hand.

"Cook. I think I can cook better than Purdy, and the first thing I would do is call somebody and make it a law that you can't serve creamed corn to anybody."

"I'd probably vote for that law, too."

He finished his dinner and Melanie watched, not having had this much fun in ages.

She went to push her hair behind her ear and realized she'd cut it off for the short look. The habit had been there for so long she did it out of instinct. *He'd* liked long hair. "What about government?"

Confusion, then total confusion wrinkled his face. "What did you say?"

"You could be a politician."

His face went blank. "That's the first time I think you're making fun of me." He got up and took his plate to the kitchen.

Melanie's face got hot and she hopped out of her seat. "No, Rolland. I would never do that to you. Never. You have a disability, but you're so much farther ahead than other people, I'm personally amazed at your progress. The fact that you can walk, and talk, and sing, and tease me…it's a blessing. I would never, ever make fun of you."

He looked at her as if his eyes were his truth meter, and they were. The huge brown depths seemed to swallow her whole. "Okay."

"Okay? I'm sorry. Do you want to play a game or turn in early?"

"I think I'll turn in—"

The doorbell rang and Rolland looked at the ceiling, then he grabbed his ears. Melanie took off for the door.

"Please, stop! He can't handle the doorbell." Melanie saw the couple on the porch and their smiles changed from happy to concerned. They pulled the door open and came in as she ran back to the kitchen. Rolland had his palms pressed against his forehead.

"Is it a migraine?" the woman asked in a hushed tone, having followed Melanie. She was rinsing a cool cloth and pressing it to the back of his neck.

"Something like that." Melanie guided Rolland to the sofa and made him sit down.

"I'm Jacquie and this is my husband, Todd. We're Scott and Heather's neighbors from next door."

"Melanie Wysh and Rolland Jones. Scott loaned us his place. Rolland, has the pain gone away?"

He shook his head no. "It's still ringing, Mel."

"Do you have any medication in your room?"

He nodded.

"Todd, go get it," Jacquie said. "Which room?"

"Top of the stairs on the right."

"Jack's room," he said and took the stairs two at a time.

"I'll get some water." The phone rang and Jacquie called, "I've got it. Hello? Hey, Scott, no, you didn't dial wrong. I'm at your house. Everything is…well, no. Not fine. Rolland's got a headache. Hold on. Here's Mel."

Melanie took the phone and Jacquie pressed the cloth to Rolland's neck and began to massage him. Todd returned with the pills and came into the kitchen for water. Melanie signaled she was stepping into the dining room for a second.

"Hi, Scott."

"Melanie, what's going on?"

"The doorbell triggered a major headache. The neighbors popped by and as soon as they rang the bell, Rolland shoved his hands to his ears and now the headache."

Scott blew out a breath. "Okay, after we talk I'll have Todd disconnect the darned thing. How's everything else?"

"Scott, he's amazing. He learned west and east today. Interestingly, I'll be looking to see how the headache affects what he's learned. Otherwise, he's been very good."

"Glad to hear it. How are you?"

"I'm fine. He tried to run me to death on the beach today. He and Horace had a great routine going and Rolland is quite strong." She said the words while wanting to get back to him.

"Yeah, Horace produces great results. Well, let me

speak to Todd. Good work, Melanie. But, if his headache worsens, he goes immediately to the hospital and is transferred to Summit. Understood?"

She was grateful he kept it short. "Yes. Thank you, sir. Todd?" she called. "Scott would like to speak to you."

Once he was done talking, he handed the phone to Melanie. Todd was about Scott's height, five-ten and had blond hair. He looked worried, yet eager to help.

"Todd, I know this is a terrible way to meet, but Scott and I are old friends. Rolland will probably be fine."

"I'm relieved. I didn't realize something we'd done caused his episode. Scott would like me to disconnect the doorbell, but I've got to run home for my tools. The kids are there. It's not quiet, but if he feels like walking over to our place, we can all go together and then walk back in a little while. Fresh air might do him good."

"Is it easing a bit, Rolland?" Jacquie asked, totally unflustered. Melanie got a good feeling about the couple.

"Yes, it's getting better."

Jacquie gave Melanie a reassuring smile. "Let's go next door then."

Melanie walked back into the great room and knelt down. "Hi, there. How about we start moving?" His eyes had been closed and when he opened them, they were bloodshot and tired looking. Rolland stood and Melanie went up under one arm and Jacquie under the other.

"What do you think you're doing?" he asked, a gentle smile on his lips. How she wanted to caress his cheek and tell him he was going to be alright.

"I'm helping you." She settled for the kind words

because they were appropriate, but wanted to say so much more.

Jacquie was again reassuring in her gaze and in her hold on Rolland's waist. Melanie gripped him, too. They moved in a slow procession with Todd leading the way.

The walk over took less than five minutes, and Jacquie talked the whole way. "Rolland, you're a tall man or I'm a midget. How tall are you?"

"I'd say six-two."

"You're not sure?"

"Not today."

Jacquie looked at him and then burst out laughing. "I'm not sure I'm thirty-seven, either. Every year I erase a couple years."

"Why?" Rolland asked.

"Because if she turns forty, she thinks her life is over, that's why," Todd said, shaking his head.

They walked through the sand and up to a gated deck where Todd punched in a code. A cool breeze licked at the trees and played fancy with the leaves. Melanie held on to Rolland's waist, her chest full of emotion. She wanted him to be okay. Didn't want him to be taken away and put somewhere else. She knew she could help him.

"Please excuse the mess," Jacquie said. "We're not housekeepers and that's all we've got to say on that matter."

"Don't worry. We're glad you can take care of the doorbell," Melanie told them.

Todd unlocked the door and they all stepped in. Todd excused himself and walked up a staircase by the wall.

Jacquie was right. Clothes were strewn over the backs of chairs and chenille blankets covered the sofa as if their owners had dashed off to return shortly. Shoes filled a blue tub and the TV was on mute, where a happy girl sang in what looked like a high school concert.

"Mommy! I missed you."

A little blond girl about three came running toward her mother and leaped. Melanie stared in surprise as Jacquie caught the child midair. "You crazy bedbug," Jacquie said. "You don't have your fairy wings. Haven't I told you that?"

She giggled. "I have one, Mommy." She held her hand out to Rolland. "I'm Lucy. What's your name?"

"Rolland."

"Is that your girlfriend?"

He looked at Jacquie. "No. That's your mom."

"Not her, silly. *Her*."

All the air in Melanie's body felt as if it were caught in her throat. Melanie moved to deny Lucy's query as Rolland shook Lucy's little hand. "No, she's not my girlfriend. I've got a headache, Lucy."

"Oh no." She scrambled out of her mother's arms. "I've got some Band-Aids. I'll get them."

"He doesn't need a Band-Aid," Jacquie told her daughter as she ran up the stairs, her fingers touching each stair.

"Yes, he does." Todd walked down the stairs and Lucy hit his thigh. "Hi, Big Daddy. I'm getting Rolland a Band-Aid for his head."

"Hi, Lady Lucy." Todd shrugged his shoulders. "Rolland, I'm sorry in advance for you."

"She's really sweet."

"You think so now, Rolland. I'll have her brother come down so you can meet him and the baby, if they're up."

Jacquie patted her husband's arm and pulled him toward the sliding door. "Moths are getting in, honey. Go fix the doorbell and hurry back. I'm going to fix Rolland and Melanie a cup of hot tea." She looked at them. "Does that sound good?"

Rolland nodded. "I think I like hot tea."

Jacquie's look was quizzical. "You think? Melanie?"

She glanced up at Jacquie and then back at Rolland. "That's just fine."

Melanie extended her hand to Rolland and he clasped it. She didn't even realize what she'd done until their fingers were locked. "Rolland, want me to massage your shoulders?"

"No. I like holding your hand. My head feels like sparklers are in it, but not so bright. The medicine is working."

"Have you had headaches like this before?"

His eyes were closed as he nodded. "Not just from one sound. It sounded like a—" he seemed to drift off and she contemplated how to disentangle their fingers. "Guitar."

"Oh."

"An electric guitar."

She looked at him oddly. "What's your mother's name?"

"Lois."

Melanie's heart raced. "Do you remember her last name?"

His head lolled to the side. "No."

"What's your name?"

"It's Rolland, silly Melanie, and I'm Lucy." The little girl was back, carrying a box of bandages.

He opened his eyes and they were cloudy. "It's Rolland, but that's not really it. I don't know."

"Lucy?" A young man called in a tolerant voice. "I think someone is going to have to sit on the stairs if she doesn't bring the Band-Aids back."

"I need them for Rolland. He has an owie."

"You cannot rename your dolls," he said, coming down the stairs with a baby in his arms. Then he saw Melanie and Rolland. "Oh, my bad. I'm Chase and this little guy is Cooper."

Lucy had changed into purple pajamas bottoms and a pink top and climbed onto the arm of the chair Rolland sat in and started putting Band-Aids on his forehead.

"Cooper is always sleeping." Chase started to say something to Lucy, but stopped. He was all teenager. Legs, baggy shorts and T-shirt.

"We have to be quiet, but he doesn't mind if we talk in a quiet voice," Lucy explained.

"You don't have a quiet voice," Chase said to his little sister.

Lucy shrugged as Melanie smiled at the siblings. She hadn't seen her own sisters, Deborah and Shannon, in seven years. She'd seen Axel, her brother, by accident three years ago, but when he'd tried to reestablish a relationship, Deion had made it clear they weren't interested.

Now she couldn't go back. She'd allowed the relationships to be severed. But she missed them. She missed the memories of those times.

Her attention went back to the baby because there was one obvious thing that was different about him and them. He was black and they were all white. "Your mom and dad adopted Cooper?"

"Yeah, and he's officially ours now. He's a cool little dude." Chase looked at his little brother with tender eyes that nearly brought Melanie to tears.

"How old are you, Chase?"

"Seventeen. Lucy is, how old, Luce?"

"Thirty-three minus thirty."

He shook his head at his sister.

"You know how people say she's a handful," Chase said.

Melanie nodded as Rolland stuck out his arm for more Band-Aids. "Mind if I hold him," Rolland asked Chase.

"Oh no," Melanie jumped in.

"Sure." Chase walked over. "Cooper's a dude's dude."

"You have a headache," Melanie reminded Rolland.

"I don't think he can catch it," Rolland said.

She felt like a complete idiot because she couldn't refute him. But what if he dropped the baby? She tried to position herself on the sofa next to Rolland, but Lucy was already there. Melanie was left to sit on the settee in front of him as Chase got the baby snuggled into Rolland's arms. Cooper smiled. "See, Mel. He likes me."

Tears filled her eyes and she couldn't stop herself from hovering. "Yeah. I see. Okay. That's enough. Our tea is here. Chase, take the baby."

"Mel, he's happy. I'll hold him just another minute, okay?"

Jacquie walked in and saw the male bonding. She handed Melanie her tea and held the tray while she sweetened it. "I love to see a man holding a baby. I heard Chase tell you we adopted him. He is definitely our little blessing. Do you two have children?"

"What? No, no. We don't. We're not together." Melanie shook her head and felt the sizzle of the tea running onto her fingers. She steadied the cup and swabbed her fingers with the napkin.

Jacquie set the tray on the table and carefully picked up Cooper, rocking him. She kissed his cheek and snuggled him to her. "Melanie, want to hold him?"

She could hardly say no when everyone was staring at her, even Lucy. "Sure. Here," she said to Rolland, giving him the tea. He sipped it. She hadn't expected that, but found she didn't mind.

As soon as the baby filled her arms, Rolland sat beside her. All that she'd been missing seemed to fall into place. Her heart was full, her body felt right. She wanted to hum and rock the baby and tell him all about her and his father. His grandmother and his grandfather. She wanted to fill him with a sense of herself and himself. But he wasn't hers. Still the feelings didn't leave. She looked at Jacquie and she nodded understanding without really knowing what was going on in her mind.

Cooper yawned and passed gas and everyone laughed. But Melanie didn't care. She was in love. "He's just wonderful. How old is he?" she said, not caring that her tears dropped onto his blanket. Jacquie came over and rubbed her back.

"Five months. Can you handle him for a little while? I'd like to have some mommy time with this angel." Jacquie sat on the couch and pulled a blanket over Lucy who snuggled with her mother.

"Sure." Melanie relaxed and Rolland gently thumbed away her tears.

"Wow. He really doesn't mind noise." Cooper slept, oblivious to the goings-on of his family.

"He'll sleep through anything, Melanie. This motor-mouth, or me playing Guitar Hero," Chase told her.

Lucy waved her hand at her brother, but looked like she was glad to have her mommy's attention.

"Jacquie, you have the perfect family," Rolland said.

"Wait, Mommy. I'll be right back." Lucy got down and put a Band-Aid on Melanie's hand.

"Honey, I'm okay."

"You're crying. You have an owie like your boyfriend."

Melanie wiped her damp cheeks. "Thank you, Lucy. You're really sweet to share with us."

"You're welcome, dear."

Melanie chuckled at the little girl. "You're such an old soul. How old are you again?"

"Three, but I'll be four in two days. Wanna come to my party? We're gonna have swimsuits and cake."

"Sounds like fun," Rolland said.

"Rolland, we're having games, too. You have to run and skip and jump." She climbed into her mother's lap and covered her legs with the blanket.

"Count me in, but not Melanie. She doesn't like to run." His arm supported Melanie's back and she nudged him. She wanted to put her head on his shoulder.

"Hey, you're not supposed to tell."

He just grinned at her.

Lucy patted his mother's arm. "Mommy doesn't either. She stays on the deck and says 'go, baby, go.'"

Jacquie shook her head. "Out of the mouth of babes."

Rolland drank their tea and Melanie stared at beautiful Cooper. He was round and bald and didn't make a sound. "Cooper is so tiny. I can't remember ever being next to a baby so small." Rolland studied him intently.

"What are you going to be when you grow up?" Melanie asked Lucy.

"A doctor. I already have Band-Aids and I can do surgery."

"No, you can't," her brother and mother said firmly.

Lucy shook her head, but didn't say anything.

Todd walked in and Lucy saw him. "Big Daddy, Cooper is gassing again."

"I'll let Mommy take care of it." He gave his wife a sly smile to show he was kidding.

Cooper's eyes opened at the sound of Todd's voice and he smiled. "Todd, I think he knows you're home," Melanie said, amazed at the baby's reaction.

"He knows, all right. He wants to hang out watching

TV all night while the rest of us sleep. I've told his brother not to let him sleep all day."

"I'm a teenager, Dad—I sleep all day. So Cooper sleeps with his big bro." Chase took off up the stairs.

Todd set his toolbox aside and sipped his wife's tea before taking the now-animated Cooper. "The doorbell is disconnected. How's your head, Rolland?"

"Much better. Thanks. I appreciate everything, but I think it's time for bed. I'm used to turning in early at Ryder."

"Oh, you're a patient?" Jacquie asked.

"I was. Mel's helping me return to the world. Thanks again."

Jacquie laid the now-sleeping Lucy on the couch. "I'm so sorry, Melanie. I thought you two were a couple. You're so perfect. I just assumed. Well, it's nice to meet you and if you need anything, please let us know." She assessed them as her husband looked on from the sofa. "You just look like you belong together."

Rolland looked down at Melanie. "Maybe one day," he said.

"Good night and thanks," Melanie said, and they stepped out into the night.

Stepping off the deck into the sand, Melanie wished this could have been a night a year ago with her husband, the man who she'd thought loved her, and their family. In their yard, with the pond she'd built.

They owned a summer home in North Carolina that was now all hers. She'd tried to wrap her mind around selling it, but her thoughts couldn't progress that far;

moving here had been all she could handle. This was too much. Rolland, the nice neighbors and Cooper. Even Lucy had been unexpectedly adorable. All the things she'd wanted in her life. She wanted to dive into her pillow for a good cry, but she had a man in her hands and no matter how hard she tried, she couldn't let go of him.

They reached the back door and were hidden by the night and the tapestry of the deck umbrella. She felt Rolland's hand on her arm and her thoughts skidded all across the star-kissed sky. She was so close to him that an escape was impossible.

"For a few minutes tonight, I felt like I'd known you before and that I should know you again. Why do I feel that way, Melanie?"

"It happens that way, Rolland. We've had a long two days."

"But you felt familiar when you were sitting next to me. Like you belonged on my arm. Was that normal?"

"I guess, Rolland."

"They said I would have muscle memory." He gazed down at her. "Give me one good reason why I shouldn't get to know you better."

Tears he couldn't see welled in her eyes and spilled. "We can't, Rolland."

"That's not good enough," he said and his lips met hers.

Their kiss was tender, as soft as the tumbling breeze that parted the leaves. Her protests were swept away with the wind. In her flat shoes she went up on her toes and pressed her lips a little more firmly into his and his heart rate sped up against her palm. He reached around and caught her in a big hug that would have made her sell all of her cashmere sweaters to have him for a lifetime.

His lips found her palm and then he let go. "We'd better say good night before we get into trouble."

"You're right, of course."

Melanie opened the door and they walked inside. "You head up. I'll get the lights in the kitchen and set the alarm."

"I'll wait. Besides, I want to know the code in case you don't want to run in the morning."

"I'm running. I don't want you leaving without me. I need to know where you are, Rolland."

"I walked the entire Ryder campus every day and made it to every one of my appointments without missing. You have to learn to trust me."

"I will," she said, "but tonight scared me. If you got a headache on the beach and I didn't know where you were, or you didn't know how to tell someone how to get you home, I'd be out of my mind with worry. Let's work on building trust, okay?"

He nodded. "Good night."

"Good night," Melanie said, before going into the kitchen, cutting off the light and letting her tears of regret fall.

Chapter Eight

Rolland ran on the beach remembering the texture of Melanie's lips. He desired them more than any physical thing, and that was saying a lot for him. He heard her calling him, but couldn't stop to give her time to catch up. She knew her way home. He needed a little private time to think. She was so desirable and her lips said yes when her mouth said no, and he couldn't figure out the difference. And there was one.

"Rolland! Wait. Please."

He turned around and there she was, running full speed toward him, her arms out too far, her stride uneven. Her form was all wrong, but she was trying, he had to give her that.

He just wished she was running to him because she wanted him the way he wanted her.

She huffed and puffed and stopped beside him. "You're running so fast today. Is something wrong?" she asked. She looked up at him, assessing, her chest rising and falling. He had to look away. There was a broken canoe ahead and he focused on it for a few moments until he could catch his breath. Maybe if he didn't look her in the face. "I'm fine. Just ready to get back and get to work," he said, looking at the top of her hair. "You okay?"

She stepped into his line of vision, her arms out, looking like she wanted to swallow her tongue. "Yes, I'm fine. You mind if we walk for five minutes?"

"No."

Rolland picked a steep sand dune and headed for it. He could almost hear Melanie groan, but he needed to find something to climb. Being around her left him with a lot of male energy that needed to go somewhere. If she wasn't always around asking if he was okay, he could take care of his situation, but she was constantly…inconveniently around.

And when she was, there were times when his desire peaked. This was one of them. He dug into the sand with both feet and climbed higher knowing she was five feet behind him.

"Okay, Rolland. I surrender."

He turned around to find Melanie's arms flapping like a windmill behind her. "I give up. I can't run anymore. I can't climb another hill with you and I'm incapable of doing…any more than collapsing." He caught her by the tail of her shirt and she plopped down on her bottom and fell backwards. "I'll fix you terrible chocolate cake if you don't ever make me climb this thing again."

He didn't feel bad for her. His discomfort was just as difficult. She jerked up as two little boys ran down the hill beside her and kicked sand in her hair. She stared at him, her face blank.

"What are you thinking?" he asked.

"Those kids need to be on a work detail somewhere."

Their mother cleared the dune and glared at her. "I heard that."

Both Rolland and Melanie laughed as he helped her up so they could walk down the dune on the other side. "She's pretty mad."

"I'd like to think she's angry at the boys for leaving her, and the fact that they aren't yet old enough for school, but I know better. I shouldn't have been so cross."

"What was your husband like?"

Her gaze ricocheted to him, then to the boats on the water.

"Do you see the yacht? The big white boat with the red and silver stripe down the side? That probably sleeps ten to fifteen and has a full-size galley. They have a sundeck with a hot tub, and with the size of that boat, there may even be a dance floor, playroom and beauty parlor on there. That's one really nice boat."

"So, he was fat?"

Melanie looked up at Rolland to see if he was teasing her. He wasn't. "No, he thought big. He liked to live big."

"You didn't. You liked to live in one room like that man?" A man in a speedboat zoomed by, jumping waves, looking like he was having the time of his life.

"No, I just didn't need big and fancy to complete me."

"But he did?"

"Yes. No." She felt frustration building. "I don't want to portray him the wrong way. He was a good man. We just didn't see eye-to-eye on living so big. I loved him, and he loved me."

"So what happened? You're confusing me. He loved you, but he divorced you. Did he find someone else?"

"I hope not. Probably. He needed a woman to be with him because he felt it made him whole. So…" She shrugged. "He probably did find someone. Maybe that's what drove him away and what drove him to divorce me."

They were at the water's edge and Rolland picked up a handful of rocks.

"You care even though you're divorced?"

"Of course. I never imagined him with anyone else."

"So his big lifestyle didn't fit you."

"No, I didn't fit him. I didn't know how to have fun. I sucked the joy out of life for him and I realize that now. I wanted things as I knew them. Simple and enjoyable. He liked things large and eccentric and magnificent."

"So what about you?" Rolland stepped in front of her and filled her hands with flat stones from the shore. "You're pretty. You can find someone else."

"I guess I never really thought about it."

He picked up some stones and skipped them in the water. She tried and the first one landed two feet ahead of her in the dirt.

She didn't say she hadn't wanted to find anyone else. That she'd thought their love had been perfect. Melanie watched his form and tried again and her rock skated against the surface two hops before plunking beneath the water. "I did it. I did it!"

"I saw you. Try again. Put your finger here on the edge of the rock."

Melanie followed his instructions and the rock skipped four times. She thrust her arms into the air and made sounds of the crowd. "I'm awesome."

Rolland watched her, smiling. "You are awesome."

"Come on, we've got work to do."

"We've been working, Melanie. Your list had something on there about wrist and hands. That's what we're using."

She gave him a knowing grin. "Ha, you think you know everything. I've got cards in my pocket. We're going to work on the beach today and do our numbers."

"Don't forget I've got plans with my friend from next door."

"I won't."

They walked to a shady portion of the beach where the overhang was about four feet. Rolland got down and started piling up sand. "What are you doing?"

"Making a backrest."

"Oh. Can I have one, too?"

"Sorry, lady. You've got to make your own."

"Is that nice?" She asked, relaxed for the first time since he'd kissed her the night before. She was glad they were away from Ryder. Glad they could be normal. Sure, she was bothered by the kiss, but in some ways she wasn't. She'd been thrilled by it. Captivated by his desire for her and even though she knew it could never happen again, she was glad to have experienced it, if only for that moment.

She got down next to Rolland and started pushing sand into a large form.

"Mel, I'm building this for you."

Her heart fluttered. "Thank you. I was just adding on so we could share."

Their gazes met and held for a moment. She looked away first and continued to pack in sand. Soon their new sofa was complete. "Want to try it out?" he asked.

She brushed off her hands and rubbed them on her thighs. "Why not."

Sitting down, she leaned back and then patted the space beside her. "Come on, let's get to work."

"Mel, what did he look like?"

"Why are you obsessed with my husband?"

"Your ex? I want to know what my competition is."

"What?" He surprised even her as she laughed. His thoughts were manly and...flattering.

"Ouch." He frowned while smiling. "I'm not good looking enough, or is it the brain injury that would take me out of the running?"

"Rolland," she moved over to give herself some

space. "There's no running. I can't get with you because it's unethical."

"Not after I finish treatment in three weeks, Mel. That's how many days?"

"You tell me. One week is seven days."

Rolland closed his eyes and she had the overwhelming urge to take his face between her hands and kiss his nose. She didn't though. She held up seven fingers, so when he opened his eyes, he'd have something to focus on.

"Fourteen."

"Plus seven more."

His eyes closed again. "Twenty-one days. That's not long at all. I'm going to find out about my life and then if I made a mess of things, or if I'm totally wrong and there's nobody waiting for me, I intend to make you fall in love with me."

"I'm not sure that's possible."

"He made you fall out of love with him."

He'd never spoken truer words. "Rolland, life isn't that simple. I tried to get him to be another type of man and that was wrong. If I could do it all over again, I wouldn't push him that way. I would try to love him for who he was."

"There's only one problem."

"What's that?"

"Who would be loving you for who you are? You act like you don't matter, Melanie, and Horace's wife doesn't act like that. She got on him for working so many late nights and early days. He told her it was because of me and that I was busted up. But she said their marriage had to come first and there was always going to be a me. I don't know what that means, but Horace started leaving on time last month."

Melanie fingered the rocks in her hand. "She meant there was always going to be a special patient. And he didn't leave you until you were out of the woods. Meaning you were in good shape before he started leaving on time."

"So, I'm in good shape?"

"You know you are."

"Good enough to date?"

"Why are you so concerned about that?" She looked at the sand, her feet. Anywhere but at him.

"Because, Melanie, you're the first person I've felt anything for. That's important. So, what does he look like? I'll bet Bugs Bunny?"

She nodded. "That's right. Skinny with bucked teeth."

Rolland didn't smile. "I've got him beat already. My teeth are new."

She laughed. "You crack me up. They are pretty."

"Okay, what else, Mel? Is he short?"

She nodded again. "Really short."

Rolland rubbed his hands together. "What else? Does he have little feet?"

She put her chin on her knees and nodded. "Uh-huh."

"And no hair, I'll bet?"

"No, none."

He looked at her out of the side of his eyes. "All right, so you," he pointed at her. "Pretty Melanie Wysh, went for a really short, bucked-teeth, little-feet man with no hair."

She pulled her lips inside her mouth and nodded. "Uh-huh."

He threw rocks at the water. "I'd have divorced you, too. You don't use good judgment. He's ugly."

Melanie couldn't help herself, she laughed so hard she fell over.

"I know why you didn't get pregnant. Your ovaries were saying hell naw. Not him."

Melanie put her face in her shirt and composed herself. "Enough out of you, Mr. Funnyman. Can we get to work, please?"

"Yes, I'm glad to know my competition is a rat. I'm focused on the goal. I need to learn how to drive. Where are the cards?"

She dug them out of her pocket and untied her jacket from her waist.

Rolland watched with rapt interest as she spread the jacket out. "Put your legs here so it won't blow away."

"I like your shirt." She'd simply added a few modifications to the T-shirt by tying it on both sides to make it fit her body better.

Melanie smiled at him. "Thanks. Now focus."

"What did you do to it?"

"A little nip-tucking here and there after I received some constructive criticism from a friend yesterday," she explained.

"You're so cute when you're embarrassed."

"I can't believe you've retained so many words. Most patients with TBI can't speak or have to relearn to swallow. But you're leap years ahead of them." She shuffled the cards and Rolland started laughing.

"What's so funny?"

"The sound the cards make. Doesn't it make you want to laugh? Do it again."

She shuffled and he cracked up again. This time she laughed, too. "No, it doesn't."

"You're laughing."

"I'm laughing at you, silly. You're so adorable." Her breath caught and the cards flew up into the air. "I didn't mean to say that."

"You said it. You can't take it back. I'm keeping it forever. I'm adorable. How tall am I, Melanie?"

"Six-two."

"I'm Rolland Jones, my mother's name is Lois, I'm six-two and I'm adorable. What's your mom's name?"

"It was Cissy. She died eight years ago."

"I'm sorry, Mel. Did you look like her?"

"No my sister Bacon does."

"Bacon? Like we get in the cafeteria on Sunday? Bacon?"

"Yes, it's really Shannon, but we used to call her Bacon. We called her Bacon because she once ate a whole pound of it before we got downstairs for breakfast. She got a whooping that day."

Melanie gathered the scattered cards and showed Rolland the first one. "This is a three and it rhymes with knee and you can see that this is a three. Say it with me."

Melanie watched Rolland practice his numbers as she walked on the beach absorbing the fading sun. He'd actually remembered three numbers for two hours. If he woke up with the same recognition, she'd silently jump for joy. He'd been tracing them with his finger, but insisted on having paper and pencil an hour ago. Their sand couch had long ago crumpled and she'd given up on rebuilding, but Rolland had wanted to rebuild, taking five minutes of patient time to compact the sand so that they'd be comfortable.

Deion wouldn't have built a sand couch, much less sat on the sand. Not for ten minutes, much less all day.

A droplet of rain smacked her calf and she looked at her leg. They'd spent all day outside and she hadn't meant to, but she'd had fun.

Walking back, she spotted Rolland looking up into the sky. "It's raining, Mel."

"I know."

A raindrop slapped him right in the face. "Ow."

"Well, don't look at it."

"Why not?"

She shrugged. "So you don't get hit."

"The rain will go around me?"

"You know it won't, right?"

"I know. I was wondering if you did." He started laughing and took off running. "Race you."

Melanie ran until she saw Rolland stop on the beach at the gate to their house. "You cheated. You had a head start. What are you looking at?"

"Look."

He pointed to a Ferris wheel off in the distance about a half mile down the beach. All the houses leading up to it were half lit, meaning the occupants were at the carnival. "Rolland, I don't think it's a good idea. First, it's about to rain and second, because of the noise factor."

"I like noise."

"Not after the doorbell incident last night. Come on inside."

"Aw, Mel. Doesn't that look like fun?"

The Ferris wheel twinkled and did look like a great time, but she didn't want to chance it. She'd long gotten over her fascination with carnivals. Deion hadn't liked them. He considered them a lawsuit waiting to happen. She had loved going as a child with her brother and sisters. Her father used to take them and they'd stand at the cotton candy machine watching as pink fluffy swirls of candy were twirled onto the paper stick.

She felt motherly taking Rolland's arm, and when he wouldn't come, she took his hand and guided him into the house. "Looks like a lot of fun. Come on inside and let's watch *Wheel of Fortune*."

"Maybe we can go down during the day when nobody is there."

"I think the noise level is still the same."

"I didn't hear them today."

"Aren't you hungry?"

"Don't do that."

"What?" She walked into the kitchen where she washed and dried her hands.

"Treat me like a child. You're distracting me."

She put her hand on her hip. "Rolland, carnivals are

typically noisy. What's going to happen when we go down there, and you—at six-two, two-hundred-ten pounds of man—have an episode and go down? What am I supposed to do as your therapist? Last night the situation was contained because we were here, and there were two other people who were nice enough and calm enough to help. But if we're at a carnival with strangers, hundreds of them and someone sees you struggling and doesn't know your situation, what's going to happen?"

He put his finger to the middle of his forehead. "Just like if a person has a heart attack or seizure, or diabete—" he took a moment. "Diabet—attack. People learn how to deal with it. People with my type of injury don't have to stay in their houses or Ryder forever, Melanie. You should know better than anyone. You should be the first one saying let's go and show the world how to deal with me." His forehead was creased in frustration, but she'd understood exactly what he meant.

"I'm sorry if I gave you that impression. But we're just learning your sensitivities. The carnival isn't a controlled environment."

"I don't know what that means. Does that mean we have to stay in because you're scared?"

Melanie remembered the time when she was little and the iron had fallen on her hand. This felt the same. He'd thrown her fear into her face and made her look at herself. Of course she was supposed to help him deal with every situation. But he was pushing her fear in her face and she couldn't tell him to back off. He had a right to answers. "We have to be cautious." *And smart.*

"I want to go back to Ryder. I'll go pack."

"What?"

"When I was in the hospital in Vegas, they kept telling me they were taking a chance on me, so I had to take a chance on them. Dr. Skerrit and Dr. Lamont. Everybody who has helped me get better has taken chances, except you. Fear surrounds you. If you're afraid, then I'll be afraid and I can't start getting scared now. I don't want to."

"I'm not afraid, Rolland."

"You're afraid to like me."

"That's different. I'm a professional."

"You're a woman first, Melanie."

His words stimulated her as if he'd told her she was the prettiest woman in the world. They were fighting and she was still attracted to him. This had to end. Maybe it was better this way. "Rolland, I have to have your well-being as my first priority. I need for you to understand that."

"Your fear is like a rock. No, it's bigger. A mountain is a rock, isn't it?"

She nodded through the tears clouding her eyes.

His quiet honesty was beating her. "Your fear is that big, Mel. You don't know what's down the beach, but something might happen. I don't know why I was in Vegas. But I don't think I was there for a good reason. I don't have a family anymore and I desperately want to know why. In the meantime, I've met someone who won't like me because rules say she can't. Otherwise you would, wouldn't you?"

She couldn't answer him.

"Tell me."

She closed her eyes and nodded, and the tears slid down her cheeks.

"That isn't supposed to hurt, but it does. You're not supposed to cry because you like somebody. I'm packing. I'll be ready in ten minutes."

He walked through the kitchen and great room, then up the stairs.

Melanie sat in the dining room trying to compose herself. *Her fear was like a mountain.* She thought she'd cried all the tears she could in a year months ago, but her body surprised her and as rain pelted the house, her thighs were bathed in tears. She let them come, staring, trying to understand why she was afraid, and why he was so smart.

Rolland in all his simplicity was digging into her secret places and shining Kentucky's fresh sunlight on them. Shaking out her dusty corners and letting her know her skeletons weren't attractive and needed to be buried. She needed to walk in the rain to the carnival and learn a little about life. A million what-ifs beat her body and she took the punches, shaking her head as her brain worked out all the scenarios. She was scared. She didn't have a lifeline. Deion was gone. Mama was gone. And Rolland was threatening to leave. But she had the chance to salvage that relationship...

Wiping her eyes, she got up and walked up the stair-case. Rolland was walking out of the room, his bags in his hands.

"I really would like for you to give me another

chance. I have no right to treat you like a child and I won't make a mistake and do it again. I won't lock you in and put the alarm on. I really want to help you, if you would just please give me another chance."

A couple seconds passed. "Okay, Mel."

He opened his door and put his bags inside. The pressure in her chest lessened. He came back out and handed her a washcloth for her face. She quickly wiped her eyes, but it didn't matter because more tears came anyway.

Rolland sat on the top stair and she sat below him and cried for a few seconds, then made herself stop.

"That's really good," he said.

"What?"

"That you can stop crying like that."

A wet sob broke out of her. "I cried a lot this year, so I decided I wasn't going to cry anymore."

He looked around the hallway. "Women are kind of strange. Men say they don't cry and we do, but we don't want y'all to know. Women cry all the time and then you stop," he snapped his fingers, "just like that."

He dug in his pocket, then held out his hand. She'd held that hand a lot lately.

"What's in there?" she asked, still shaking a bit from her tears.

"You have to open it and see."

Melanie felt herself smiling and uncurled his fingers. He held a Mini Snickers bar.

"How did you know I love these?" She took it, looking at him and tearing it open with her teeth. Snaking her tongue inside she used her fingers to push the candy into her mouth.

"Thank you, Rolland."

"My pleasure."

A tantalizing thrill raced up her back.

"What about your pleasure, Melanie?"

She finished her candy and looked directly at him. "We're going to have to deal with it. I don't know how, Rolland. Ethics say no, and I don't want to lose the first job I've had in years. And the woman in me is…feeling like the man in you."

He reached out and stroked her cheek.

She closed her eyes and accepted his caress. "But that's as far as it can go."

Chapter Nine

Rolland wished he could remember how to write the number three, but he couldn't. If he saw it, then he remembered what it looked like, but he couldn't write it. He hated it. He put down his tracing pad and went out on the deck. The day was cool, the air blowing in off the water, and he had to wear long pants, too. He hated long pants. Today wasn't looking like a great day. Kentucky in September was turning cold.

Todd came out of his house with wood and a hammer and Rolland felt himself smiling. "What you got there?"

"Lucianna wants to have a lemonade stand before her birthday party. I told her everyone is going to the carnival and she's not going to get any customers, but she doesn't care, so I'm building her one."

Rolland smiled. "You called her Lucianna."

"Yes, that is her Christian name, but her nickname is Lucy."

He thought about it for a moment. "I get it. Do you need help?"

"Sure do. Chase and Cooper are up there sleeping for a few more hours," Todd said and nodded him over. "Come on."

"Hold on." Rolland ran to the back door and opened it. "Mel, I'm heading next door to help Todd. Mel!"

"In the laundry room. Hold on. Yes?" She popped from around the corner.

"I'm heading next door to help Todd make lemonade. See you later."

"What?"

"I'll be back, woman. I'm going to do man's work," he said in his special voice.

"Bye." She laughed.

Rolland hammered away and after awhile, Todd stopped him for the tenth time. "Have you ever hammered before?"

"I don't know, but it's fun."

Todd laughed. "Yeah, but we need the wood to be in good shape for her to use it, my friend, or else it's sawdust. Hold on, I think we'd better put these goggles on you."

"With the bike helmet, too?"

Todd nodded, already covered up. "Yeah, we can't be too careful. Now, you're looking smart," he complimented. "Now this nail goes in here, and this time, no thumb."

Rolland raised the hammer high and Todd stopped him. "Remember, we're making this for a four-year-old. We want it to be sturdy, but we have only five nails left."

"You're right. A lower stroke is all we need." He got the nail in quickly, and Todd placed the last nails. Soon they were on to sanding.

"Rolland, tell me your story."

"I was in an accident and don't have a memory for a good portion of my life. I'm trying to get it back, but it's not coming. I have to relearn things and Melanie is teaching me. So, Todd, what are you getting Lucy for her birthday?"

"A car."

He stared, open-mouthed. "A little girl can drive?"

Todd's laugh shook his shoulders and his neck. "No. Well, yes. In a kid car. It's a small car made for children. I had this one custom-made. That's why it's not here yet. It won't be delivered for another week."

"For a child? That's like manual windows. Unbelievable."

"From anybody else, I'd get a little angry, but from you, I'm tending to agree. All this for a little girl who asked only for a lemonade stand."

"I didn't mean to make you feel bad, Todd. You're a good father. You have a good family. I've been at Ryder for months and at another hospital for months and nobody looked for me. In my other life, I probably acted and smelled like wet socks."

Todd looked at him with piercing blue eyes that grew misty. He extended his hand and Rolland shook it.

"Rolland, even if you were a not-so-great guy before, you're a good man now, and that's what counts."

"Thanks, Todd. So what does the car do?"

"Oh, it's special. The windows go up and down, the seats go forward and backward. She'll have it for a while, and then when she outgrows it, it'll go to my man Cooper. The horn works, and it can go up to ten miles per hour. Just fast enough for me to have a heart attack as I jog along beside her. Rolland, are you okay?"

"I want a car," he said earnestly.

"Buy one."

"I think I have a blue one, but Melanie says I can't drive."

"Oh, well, there's probably rules regarding driving with your condition, but after you get your head together, you can probably get your license and start driving again."

"I can't wait! I want to stick my arm out the window and wave to people, and drive around corners."

Todd patted his shoulder, grinning. "Your day will come, buddy. So what's up with Melanie?"

Rolland sanded some more. "I really like Melanie, but she won't let me kiss her. Oh, I brush my teeth two times a day, but it's because she's my therapist."

Todd stopped sanding and rested his arms on one knee. "My friend, it's a matter of ethics. She's right, but you're in luck. People break rules all the time."

Rolland smiled. "Who?"

"Senators, Congressmen. We even had a president who—"

Rolland was staring. "What'd he do?"

Todd blinked rapidly. "Doesn't matter. The point is there are ways around rules. The first thing is, does she like you?"

He nodded. "She was crying, but she said she did."

Todd looked skeptical. "That can go both ways. Was this good crying?"

"Yes, but she said we couldn't be together because of ethics, and she needs her job."

"Oh." Todd sucked air through his teeth. "A stickler for the rules. Those are the worst ones when it comes to matters of the heart. Well, you're going to have to woo her."

Rolland sanded a little more. "I'm not good at singing. I tried and we know that's not my former profession. I'm not good."

Todd's chest started shaking long before the laugh fell out of his mouth. "Okay, woo means to convince her to like you. Now you're a smart guy, even with your brains scrambled, right? Can I say that and not offend you?"

"Scrambled brains?" Rolland smiled. "That sounds about right."

"All right, then you have to win her over. Do you remember the art of winning over a woman?"

"The last date I remember having, I gave her a wrist corsage and my father had on plaid shorts and a white T-shirt. We rode in the backseat of his car and he dropped us off."

"Sad memory," Todd pointed out.

"How's the stand coming," Jacquie asked, sticking her

head into the garage. "Oh, hi, Rolland. I didn't know Todd had recruited you. I'd have warned you not to come."

"Do you want me to leave?"

"No." She looked alarmed. "Good heavens, no."

Todd got off the floor, holding his back. "Honey, we're having some male bonding time as we finish our manly project. Can you get us some of your world-famous Diet Coke?"

He then began to speak to her in French. She answered and Rolland watched with interest. Then she nodded and smiled at him before going inside.

Todd came back and got back on the ground, grunting the whole way down.

"My friend," he told Rolland, "flowers are your friend."

Rolland finished sanding. "Flowers. Okay, that's all I have to do is give Melanie flowers and she'll forget about ethics?"

Todd flipped his hand over a couple times. "Maybe some candy."

Rolland thought about it and breathed hard. "That's a problem."

"Why's that a problem?"

"She goes with me to the store. She won't let me buy her candy."

Todd clapped his hands. "I've got the answer. I'll buy the candy and you give it to her."

Rolland shook his head. "That's not good. You buying Melanie candy. What will Jacquie think? That could cause problems. What if I give you the money and you buy the candy?"

Todd nodded. "That would work. See? You're thinking ahead. I like that. Last thing. After-dinner walks."

Rolland sighed. "She's lazy. She hates running on the beach every day. Really, it's stressful."

This time, Todd's laughter started in his legs and eventually his whole body was shaking. "Rolland, you're a funny guy. I meant walk to town. The walk is nice and slow and you can stop at the café and listen to music and get a cup of tea. But the best part is that it gets dark earlier and so if you leave about six thirty, by the time you start back, the stars will be out and you can hold hands."

Rolland felt his mouth fall open. He started smiling. "Todd, I like you."

Todd stood up and flipped over the lemonade stand. "It's ready."

Rolland dusted off the table while Todd called Jacquie and the kids. Soon Lucy was set up at the end of the driveway and as she put on her lemonade hat, people came out of their houses to buy cups of her lemonade. Rolland went inside and cleaned up, anxious to get back outside. "She's making a killing, Melanie. We need to go buy some."

"I don't think she needs us."

"But I told her we'd stop by. They won't have any by the time we get there. She has a line. She needs to copyright her product and then lease the rights to a larger company. They can market and get the product on the shelves. She'd be rich by her tenth birthday."

Melanie shook his arm. "Do you hear yourself?"

"No. I was just..." He put his finger to his forehead. "Talking about lemonade, Lucy and selling her rights."

"I know. You sounded knowledgeable."

"Maybe I was some type of strategist."

Melanie's grin was encouraging. "Maybe. We've been writing numbers all day. How would you like to cook tonight?"

"Us. You and me in the kitchen together?"

"Yes. You and I in the kitchen together. What do you say?"

"Why not? Wait. Are you running out of ideas on how to cook chicken?"

They were in the dining room at the table working on the number four, but Melanie surprised him and sank her fingers into her glass of water and then flicked him.

"Whoa!" He laughed, wiping his face. "Where's the abuse coming from?"

"I thought we were friends? You're such a smarty-pants. You plan the menu from food we have in the kitchen."

"I can do that, but first I have to go into town." Rolland got up. "Come on, Melanie. You have to come, too."

"What about dinner?"

"It'll keep."

Rolland grabbed his jacket and hurried out the door and he could hear Melanie running around, grabbing her sweater and keys for the car and shutting the doors. He hurriedly snatched up a bunch of flowers from the yard but was worried that the roots were still on them.

Todd shook his head wildly from his garage, gesturing for Rolland to do something to the bottom of the flowers.

Rolland shook them.

Todd gave up and ran over. "Rolland, next time, we're going to have to talk details. The beauty is in the details."

"These look terrible. So far, Todd, your idea isn't going too hot."

"It's working now, my friend."

Todd pocketed the shears he'd used to cut off the bottom of the flowers and walked toward his daughter's lemonade stand just as Melanie was coming out of the house and locking the door. "You look nice," Rolland told her and gave her the flowers.

"Thank you." She looked so surprised. Then she looked at the obvious hole in the flower bed and didn't say anything.

They walked down the drive and she approached Lucy. "May I have a glass, please?"

"It's three dollars."

"For lemonade?" Melanie said, aghast.

"I put a lot of stuff in it," Lucy told her. "And then you have to stop by Mommy over there. She puts her own stuff in it." Lucy shrugged. "I don't know. Mine is better."

"How much for two glasses?" Melanie asked the little girl. Lucy counted on her fingers.

"I don't know. Big Daddy? They want two."

"Six dollars."

Rolland reached into his pocket and gave Lucy six dollars and Todd gave Rolland the thumbs-up.

"What's going on between you and Todd?" Melanie asked as she took the two large cups.

"Nothing. Male bonding. We built that stand," he said with pride.

"It's very nice." They headed toward Jacquie who had been talking to an older couple. When she saw them approaching, the couple waved and headed home and Jacquie joined them.

"Vodka?" she asked, and Melanie started laughing. No wonder the lemonade was so expensive. The vodka was Grey Goose.

"Sure," Rolland said, but Melanie shook her head.

"No, thanks. We're walking to town. We want to get there without falling down, right, Rolland?"

"That's a good idea. Bye, Jacquie." She headed back to her daughter and applauded when Lucy showed her all the money she had made.

"I want children so badly."

"Your husband didn't?"

"Excuse me?" Melanie said turning around and sipping her drink.

"You said you want children badly."

She looked embarrassed. "I didn't mean to say that aloud. But it's out there now. I do want children. Someday."

"Sounds like today."

She tipped her head to the side and skipped over a crack in the sidewalk. "That would be impossible. But maybe I will adopt."

He thought about it for a minute.

"What?" she asked.

"I didn't say anything."

"But you want to," she told him.

"You really deserve a baby if that's what you want. You look really great with Cooper. You fell in love, didn't you?" he asked, looking at her with sympathetic eyes.

"Yes." Melanie seemed really happy to see a streetlight and change the subject. "I know we have these on campus, but this is a trick question. What do you do if the light is flashing red?"

"You take your special friend's hand and cross the street after looking both ways." Rolland looked down at her.

They'd hit town and the crowd moved to a lazy pace, everybody strolling. The friendly atmosphere made him feel good, despite the lower temperature. An elderly lady bustled toward him in a beige trench coat and chiffon scarf around her head. He stepped to the side and let her pass, then took Melanie's hand again.

Melanie looked at the sign over the door. Café Amore. "How'd you hear about this place?"

"I was male bonding and Todd told me."

"So he's your best friend now?"

He liked that she looked kind of jealous and sounded like it, too. He'd be hanging out with Todd a little more. "No, Horace is, but if you want to be my second best friend, then Todd, that's all right with me."

"You can be his friend." Her voice was kind of high and she tried to look as if it didn't matter that she'd been washing clothes and not hammering outside with him.

She was jealous. He'd learned a lot from watching daytime TV all those weeks.

"I know that, Melanie. But I'd like it if you were my second best friend, giving Horace a run—"

He opened the door and looked down at her as she passed under his arm. "A run for what, Mel?"

"His money," she said shyly.

"A run for his money. That's right. Todd said we have to buy a drink, but we can read all the magazines we want."

The café was nothing but magazines. A tall woman with long blonde hair approached them. "Welcome to Café Amore. I'm Isabel."

"I'm Rolland and this is Melanie."

"Welcome," she said with a smile. "We have magazines to suit every pleasure. Find something you like and make yourselves comfortable. What can I get you to drink?"

"Hot chocolate," Rolland told her, and Isabel grinned up him. A guttural laugh came out of her.

"You are hot chocolate, Rolland. That's perfect for you. And you, Melanie?"

"The same, with a touch of cream."

"Again, perfect. Make yourselves comfortable. Well, the tables are taken, but the couch in the upstairs living room is open. I'll bring your drinks up there. Rolland, what do you like to read?"

"Anything with pretty women."

Isabel looked at Melanie, who shrugged her shoulders. "What can I say, he's his own man. I'll take one with handsome men."

"You two help yourselves." Thinking they were

playing a joke on her, Isabel laughed and went behind the counter to prepare their drinks.

They gathered a handful of magazines and went upstairs. Soothing, sexy jazz filtered through a clear sound system. Sitting on the comfortable sofa, Rolland looked at the other couples who were already seated in chairs made for two. Rolland took off his jacket and looked at Melanie. "I'll hang up yours if you'd like."

"Thank you. I'll hold our seat on the couch."

Melanie sat down just before another couple, who took quite a bit of space. By the time Rolland returned and sat down, they had to get close. Melanie sat by the arm of the sofa and turned so that her legs were over his. "Hi," he said. "You have pretty feet."

"Thanks," she whispered. She flipped her magazine open and started reading.

They read for a while, but he kept getting distracted. "Uh, Mel?"

"Yes?"

"Do you think she's my wife?"

For a long second her gaze held his as if to see if he was really serious. "Well, let me see."

She looked at the photo and saw the picture of Michelle Obama. "No, sweetie. That's the president's wife. You're not married to her."

"She's pretty."

Melanie nodded. "Yeah, but she's got a guy already. Keep looking."

Isabel arrived with their drinks, a vase for Melanie's

flowers and a slice of pound cake to welcome them to her store. They thanked her and she was off to help other customers.

"What about her?" Rolland asked Melanie once he got the flowers in the vase.

Melanie leaned over and looked at a photo of actress Vanessa Williams. "She's gorgeous, but I don't think so. She lives in New York and Los Angeles and she's got four children."

"I could have lived in New York and Los Angeles. I could have four children." Rolland rubbed Mel's ankle and ran his hand up to her knee. Her toes wiggled and he put his palm down there to play with them.

"You could have, but the thing about being married to a public figure is that everyone knows her. And because you've been missing for so long, she would have had people looking for you, too."

"That's true." He nodded. "If I had been your husband, would you have looked for me, Mel?"

He was so serious, it was as if the weight of the world rested on her answer. "Yes, if I'd known where to look, Rolland. I would have looked for you." She blinked a lot and reached for her hot chocolate.

"Is something in your eye?"

"No, I'm fine."

"Mel, I have a confession to make. I learned something today."

She was looking into the fireplace, staring at the orange flames.

"What is it?" She sighed as a slow song started

playing and couples started dancing. "Rolland, would you like to dance?"

"Sure. Our west-to-east dance?"

"Oh. No. I'm sorry. I just assumed you remembered how to dance."

"I can sway like they're doing. Come on," he said to stop her from going back to the couch.

Rolland took her hand and brought her into his arms. They began to move to the music and after a few awkward seconds, Melanie fit against him. "You belong right here, Mel."

Her heart beat against his hand and her hips fit against his legs. He smelled her hair and it reminded him of coconut and her perfume of flowers.

"What were you going to tell me when we were on the couch?"

"I speak French."

She looked up at him. Her expression said she didn't believe him. "You don't speak French, Rolland."

"Tue es trés belle."

"What did you say?"

"You are very beautiful. *Puis-je t'embrasser?*"

"What did you say?"

"Does it matter?" he asked.

Their gazes locked, held. *"No, mon cher."*

Their lips met and Rolland savored the gentleness of their kiss. The fact that she surrendered another piece of herself to him made him feel special inside. Her lips sought his cheek and rested there a few seconds. "Oh, Rolland," she whispered. "We're in public."

"Let them get their own girl," he said of the guys who'd just come up the stairs. Melanie put her head against his chest, and this was one time he wished he wasn't so much taller than she was. The thought was odd. He hadn't known her for that long, but he felt as if he'd danced with her before. He liked having her there against him. He liked that she hadn't run away from this beautiful moment.

"You speak French, Rolland. I didn't know you spoke French."

"I know. You called me sweetie."

She thought back to when he asked about Mrs. Obama. "I did call you sweetie. A lot of firsts for both of us."

He was looking down at her. "You can't take it back."

For a second as they danced, her hand tensed in his. Then she nodded. "I won't."

"And you have to call me sweetie in private several times a day."

"Rolland, you're pushing it." He loved when she let go and smiled.

"Wait," he whispered bringing her closer. "Laugh again so I can feel it inside of me."

"Oh my God, you're going to make me fall in love with you."

"That's my greatest wish. Let's go home."

Chapter Ten

Rolland read the measurements on the box of pancakes and looked at the cup one last time. "Melanie, it has the same one-third, I promise. You have to trust me. Did you tell me that the other day?"

"Yes, Rolland, but we have to have dinner and it's almost midnight."

"But are we starving? You can eat any of the other pancakes I made you."

She looked around the kitchen at the plates of pancakes in various states of death. There was no way she was risking her stomach on those things. "No, thanks. If you're sure."

"I'm not sure. I'm positive. One-third cup of milk. I box pancake mix."

"Rolland, can you read that one more time? I think we need to turn off the oil. It's starting to smoke again."

He hurriedly moved the frying pan off the gas burner and cut it off. "Whew, that was close. You know what, Mel?" he said with his hand on his hip. "I know I was a good cook. Maybe I was better with meat. I think you started me off in the wrong area."

"Me? Me? You're blaming me? You wanted to cook this late. I said let's grab something in town because we were already there, but no, you wanted to walk home and cook."

"Oh, no. Cooking wasn't my idea of fun. You said I had to learn how to cook. I want to hire someone to cook for us. But you don't want me to burn down the house. Do you think this would happen if someone cooked for us?"

"I'm not having this conversation at twelve-twenty in the morning. I'm going to eat the pancake batter and the bacon I cooked."

He poured in the milk and read the box. "Two cups pancake mix." He stirred in the mix and read the box. "Heat oil. This is a lot of work."

He turned on the burner and watched it heat. He picked up the box. "Pour in batter."

"No!" she said as he poured all the batter into the frying pan.

"What?" he asked. "It said pour in batter."

Melanie looked in the frying pan at the bubbling, frying cake. "Tomorrow we make peas."

"I don't like peas," he said.

"Good. Peas it is."

* * *

At one o'clock, Melanie finished cleaning the kitchen and wiped down the last cabinet. She turned off the lights in the kitchen and was surprised to see Rolland still up. His silhouette was highlighted by the floodlight from outside although he was inside the house. He'd taken his shower long ago and gone to bed she'd thought. "You still up?" she asked.

"I was waiting for you."

Her heart skipped a beat. "Why?"

"I don't know. I didn't feel right leaving you down here alone while I turned in. Didn't seem manly."

"You cooked. Only right that I clean up the kitchen."

"Tell the truth. You wanted me out of the way."

"Okay. I wanted you to stop making such a mess. I admit it." She laughed. She hadn't lied to him.

He rubbed his stomach. "I saw a man with an earring today."

"Yeah? What'd you think of that?"

"I thought, that's pretty cool. Does he get a lot of chicks with that earring?"

Mel straightened the pillows on the couch, the chairs and the books on geography on the coffee table. She didn't want to sit. They'd done a lot of that at the café and now if she sat, she'd be on top of him. Her attraction to him was that powerful.

"So, did he get a lot of chicks?"

"Yeah, two."

"So it was the earring?" she asked, standing near the

fireplace while he leaned against the back door that faced the beach.

"No, I'm sure it was the man not the earring. One was his wife and the other his daughter. But they sure looked happy."

Rolland seemed so lonesome. His yearning was so visceral that she wanted to reach inside of him and soothe all his aches. But if his memory returned as sometimes happened, he'd go back to being the man he was and nothing that happened now would matter.

"You should stop worrying so much about your past and focus on getting better. You'll have everything you want. Your life is out there and you can do with it what you want. It won't be the same, but you can have a great new life."

"Why won't it be the same? Why do you sound so sure?"

In the semidarkness she wished she hadn't said those words so emphatically. She finally crossed to him. "You have to trust me. I've seen this before and I know what I'm talking about. You're going to be fine, Rolland. In a few weeks, your life in the outside world will begin again. Where do you think you'd like to live?"

"I don't know. Where do you live?"

"Here in Kentucky."

"All your life?"

"No. I was born in Georgia, but that's neither here nor there. Have you ever wanted to see someplace or go someplace special?"

He shrugged. "I don't know."

"Well, why don't you think about it, and we can look at the map and maybe find a place you might want to go or haven't been—"

"Mel, I don't have anyone. Right now, you and the people next door, along with Horace, are my only friends. I don't want to move."

Her heart shattered. "Rolland, I'm so sorry."

"I don't want your pity."

"I don't pity you. I was insensitive."

"Why?"

"Because I wasn't really registering that you aren't like ninety-nine percent of the patients I work with. I've never had someone who's had no one."

"I see." He looked out the window. "The Ferris wheel lights just went off. I guess that's o̶ ̶ ̶ ̶ ̶ ̶ ̶ ̶ Would you do me a favor?"

"Sure, Rolland. What is it?"

"Would you call your sisters an̶ ̶ b̶r̶o̶t̶h̶e̶r̶ ̶a̶n̶d̶ ̶g̶e̶t̶ ̶ ̶ ̶ ̶ with them? It's a shame to have them and n̶o̶t̶ ̶k̶n̶o̶w̶ ̶t̶h̶e̶m̶."

The rest of the carnival lights began to extinguish. She didn't know if her family would accept an overture from her. Her chest was full, her heart pounding through her hands. She felt it in her jaw, and tried to stop clenching her teeth. "I'll think about it."

"Mel?"

She was nearly up the third stair. "Yes?"

"Don't think about it too long." His kiss against her forehead was gentle and it was she who held onto their embrace the longest.

* * *

Two weeks had passed, and Melanie paused over her journal on her lap and reread her documented entries on Rolland's progress. The entry from three days ago stated: *September 15: He spoke French today, a skill he's never demonstrated before. The first presentation was when he was visiting with the neighbors, helping construct a lemonade stand. He mentioned the couple speaking and his comprehension of their conversation. Later, he spoke French to me and I confirmed this ability.*

Mr. Jones has cognitive memory of numbers, but as of yet no written recall. Am considering alternative tools. Has reached and maintained skill level on compass. Assessment: Good. Prognosis: Excellent. On task for completion 2.5 weeks.

Melanie circled the numbers she'd written and sighed. They were still cooking and learning measurements. If all Rolland had to do was operate the microwave, he'd be fine. But sometimes, he'd have to turn on a stove and he had to know how to handle an emergency if things went wrong.

He'd had a ball at Lucy's birthday party and their surprise trip to the carnival. She couldn't help but think about how much time he'd spent playing with her. They'd won every contest beating Chase and Lucy's cousin Simon, who'd been a big cry baby according to Lucy. Simon was five and hadn't taken that very well.

Their house was still asleep and Melanie was glad to have the quiet morning to herself. She closed her eyes, snuggling deeper into her fleece jacket and wondered if she should try meditating. She'd brought her yoga mat onto the deck with her, but had left it on the chair as if avoiding the foam rubber would stop her from contemplating the direction of her life.

Nothing was stopping her, apparently. She wanted a baby so badly her subconscious thoughts had become verbal. She had let the line between ethical and unethical behavior blur, and she was flirting with—she looked up into the sky and faced her own truth—she was having real loving feelings toward Rolland.

It was time to cut and run.

Melanie ruminated on the old adage and shook her head. She never quit and she never ran. But resisting Rolland was becoming harder by the day. Heck, after two weeks in this house, by the hour.

She looked at her yoga mat with trepidation. If she got down there she would figure out what to do. Getting out of her chair, Melanie sat on the mat and started deep breathing, imagining herself going to a higher place. She cleared her head and started asking questions she dared not speak aloud. The answers flew around her and she understood with clarity, but the complications were enormous. She sought higher answers, as the sun warmed her skin and she could feel herself floating, knowing the ultimate honesty was within her.

The door to the house closed behind her and her meditative connection was broken. The calm wasn't completely gone, although Rolland was present. She didn't move, hoping he somehow understood her need for space. She felt him sit behind her on the mat. Deion would never have done that. She began to wonder what he was doing.

Thinking that he was mocking her, she turned around to confront him. Melanie's jaw relaxed when she saw him not quite in position because he wore a brace on his knee, but his other knee was bent, his hands in the *jnana mudra* position.

His eyes were closed, his head facing forward as he breathed in to the bottom of his lungs and exhaled slowly. She knew they'd taught meditation as a therapy at Ryder. She just hadn't known Rolland had taken the class. She waited quietly. He meditated for ten minutes before opening his eyes. "Good morning."

She looked at him as if she'd never seen him before. Before right and wrong could fight to the death, Melanie leaned forward and kissed him. His arms slid around her and his thick lips greeted hers as if they'd missed her for years.

"Good morning," she said, when she could speak. Rolland stood up and helped her up. He opened the door to the house and let her walk in before him, before he closed the door and the blinds.

He didn't say anything as he rolled up the mat and stood it on the staircase. Melanie wasn't sure what to do. She'd just had a serious talk with herself and with the Higher Power, and thought they'd collectively come to an understanding. She was going to behave herself during their twenty remaining days. Her temptation would be lessened.

But something had happened in the translation. Lessened had become heightened.

Rolland had her hand and he was heading for the sofa.

And now she was straddling him. He was unzipping her fleece jacket and she liked the expression on his face. She caressed his jaw and made him look into her eyes.

"We were meant to be. You know that."

Out of everything Rolland had said those words hit home. "Yeah?"

He nodded. His hands were on her waist and he shook her. She wrapped her arms around his neck and dragged her mouth across his in a kiss so good that she rose on her knees, following his mouth until his head tilted over the back of the sofa. Her tongue tangled with his, her lips caressed his, his breath becoming hers, and hers, his.

His arms wrapped her back, bringing her into him, tightly. His lips ravaged her neck in warm kisses, and when he got to her ears she nearly jumped off his lap. "Good?" he asked.

"Erogenous zone," she replied.

"That sounds sexy," he chuckled, and kissed her there again and again until she felt as if she was going to burst into flames.

Her thighs tightened against his legs as she tried to keep her head on straight. So far things hadn't gone too far. This was okay if they didn't make love. She sank her hands beneath his shirt into a nest of chest hair. She sought his nipples and ran her palms over them, and then the tips of her fingers.

"That feels good," he told her, his eyes closed.

More didn't need to be said. She kept up her effort to please him.

He claimed her mouth again, his other hand bringing

her against his sex and for a second, their lips parted. Their eyes opened. The question lingered. Would they...

Her eyebrow slid up and his eyes widened as he took her hips into his hands. He brought her against him in a slow grind of building passion. Their lips met again.

The phone rang.

Melanie tried to move, but Rolland stopped her.

"Wait. Slow down. Slow down," he said quietly. "Do you really need to get that?"

She recognized it wasn't the house phone either but her cell, which meant it could have been anyone. "I do."

She lifted her leg off his and made her way across the great room to the table where she'd plugged in her cell. "Hello?"

"Melanie, it's Cali."

"Oh, hi. How are you?"

"Fine. Where are you?"

"Why?" Dragging her hand through her hair, Melanie walked through the den, behind the couch, knowing Rolland was watching her. She didn't want to break the spell that had been cast throughout the room and over them. She didn't want her passion wasted. She wished she'd looked at the caller ID before picking up. Suspicious, Melanie unplugged the phone and took it into the kitchen and started pulling out food for breakfast. She slowly made her way into the garage before pulling the door closed behind her. "Why?" her tone was sharp and bordered on nasty, and she reined in her rare temper.

"I need to know. Melanie, I need to know where you're at."

"Cali, I'm caring for a patient. His stay and location don't need to be approved by you."

"Who do you think you're talking to?" She sounded shrill and out-of -control. "It's inappropriate for you to have driven off with a patient. No one knows where you are. Don't you think there's talk flying around here about that? I'm the only one bold enough to call you out about your behavior."

"Put Scott on. I want to know who authorized you to make this call."

"N-nobody's here at the moment, but—"

"I thought so. Once again you've overstepped your boundaries. You're going to be sorry you made this call. Scott is well aware of Rolland's whereabouts. If you have any questions you need to talk to the president, Cali, do you understand?"

"What makes you so special that you get to be alone with the richest single man ever to come to Ryder? A lot of us deserve a shot."

Melanie reared back. "You're out of line. Goodbye."

Melanie disconnected the call and stood in the cold garage, shaking. The phone fell out of her hand and shattered. Something was going on at Ryder. Otherwise, why would Cali be calling now. Scott knew she was here, but Cali could cause unnecessary attention to Rolland.

"What did she want?" Rolland asked and Melanie jumped.

"To be a pain in the behind. That's all Cali ever wants."

"Come inside. It's cold out here."

She retrieved the pieces of the phone and walked inside the house.

Rolland stood between the kitchen and dining room where they ate all their meals. The desire they'd felt simmered between them like a stew, a blend of looks and emotions and unspoken words that couldn't be separated back into individual pieces. A single stroke from either of them would have ignited the passion, but the berth they gave each other was wide. She wanted to talk to him and tell him everything, but couldn't.

She needed to help him. That was her only duty. Loving him wasn't part of her job description.

Rolland looked at her with such passionate concern she wanted to cry. She had to be strong for the both of them. He had to learn more while he was here. And she was going to teach him.

Melanie put the phone back together. "Cali's goal is to get her best friend Barbara back on the job, and my job, Rolland—" she held out both hands to him "—my job is to help you return to society as whole as possible. Are you hungry?"

He nodded.

"I'll feed you," she told him. "What do you have a taste for?"

"You. I want you."

"We're getting there, okay?"

"For real?"

She nodded. "For real."

"Let's get to work."

Chapter Eleven

Melanie's expressions grew more somber as afternoons tripped over dusk into evenings. She stopped working to cut carrots and potatoes and beef into pieces and put everything into a cooker on the counter that bubbled all day. Different days, different food, but it all bubbled.

Rolland felt as if he was boiling, too. She was irresistible as she made cards and drew on paper. They cut out letters, colored them, traced them and even wrote numbers in the sand. They ate dinners and breakfasts, and ran and kissed and ate again. She'd finally given up resisting her attraction to him. And Rolland was glad. Being with her felt natural. The only disappointment was that he retained nothing when it came to writing numbers.

Today, Melanie wore a pink velour jogging suit and

a white cotton long-sleeve top. Her hair was getting longer as the red spikes curled on top. She looked intently at some medical books on her lap after dinner one night. "Rolland, perhaps you aren't meant to know numbers but for a day at a time. Perhaps our approach has been wrong all along."

Rolland tossed the ball into the air he'd found on the beach earlier that day, catching it.

"This is a five, it sounds like hive, this is a five. This is a four, it sounds like door, this is a four. I wonder if we can make up a new rhyme that sounds like a rap or something."

Melanie sat across from him in a floral-print wing chair and all he wanted to do was throw her papers on the floor and make her not look so serious.

"Can you rap and I don't know it?" she asked.

"I don't know. Can I?"

"What's wrong with you?"

Thunder shook the house. "Nothing." He tossed the ball up and caught it. "I'm tired of being brain dead. If I have kids, they're probably worried sick about me. If I have a wife, she's probably sleeping with another man, and I'm throwing a ball into the air while you try to figure out how I'm going to remember numbers."

"You're not brain dead. You're bored and you're feeling sorry for yourself."

He sat up and tossed the ball higher. "Yes, Mel. I'm in a bad mood and I'm frustrated."

The lights flickered. "Do you want to start a fire in the fireplace before we lose the lights?" she asked.

"I guess so." Halfway to the fireplace the lights went out.

"Hold on," she said. "Let me get a flashlight."

"No, you hold on, Melanie. I'm the man in this relationship and it's time I started acting like it. Where are the flashlights?"

"In the kitchen drawer next to the refrigerator. May I say something else?"

"What?"

"You're very sexy when you're bossy."

"And it's about time you noticed!" he chuckled. It was as if she'd opened a window. A smile played on his lips. The solar night lights flickered on. "And when I get back, we're going to get on the couch and make out."

"I'm closing my books right now."

"I'll get the flashlights."

Rolland felt his way into the kitchen and made it safely to the drawer. "I've got them! I'm awesome."

"You irresistible cup of hot chocolate." Melanie giggled.

"I like that." He walked back in and gave her one of the lights, then headed over to the fireplace. "You stay on the couch. If I need your help, I'll call you."

"Okay." He liked the way she didn't argue with him, but gave him a chance to be a man and check out the fireplace himself. The instructions were simple. He turned the nozzle, pushed the buttons and the fire popped up in the fireplace. "If cavemen had this, the world would be a different place."

"A truer statement hasn't ever been said."

"That's a brain teaser."

"How do you know?" she asked as he came and sat next to her, putting her legs in his lap. He stripped off her socks and tossed them onto the floor.

"Because I had to say that phase in therapy after they fixed my mouth. Used to give me the biggest headache. I don't want to talk about me or being sick or being on the way to getting well. I'm a man and you're a woman and that's…" He slid his hands up her legs. "That's all I want to focus on. What do you like about me?"

"You're honest."

"I don't have a choice. What else?"

"No, Rolland. There is a genuine honesty about you that's so incredible, I admire that quality."

"Are you unhonest? Is that a word?"

He didn't know what demons chased her, but they had somehow found Melanie in that home and wrestled the peace out of her body. "The word is dishonest. Everyone is dishonest at times, Rolland. I am, too."

"I can't believe you'd lie about anything, Melanie."

"Not to hurt anyone, Rolland. To protect them. You asked me once what my husband looked like."

"You didn't want to tell me and you made up a whole bunch of stuff."

She took his hand and stroked his fingers. "His face wasn't ever as understanding as yours. His words never as gentle. We didn't laugh like you and I do, and we never sang badly and danced together. We belonged to a country club. That's a fancy gym where people with money go to exercise with other people who have money. But he and

I never ran in the mornings or ever." She kissed his fingertips. "We had a lot of things, but we didn't have friendship like I've known with you. He was tall and handsome, but not as good looking and kind as you."

"I'm a good catch, Mel. I don't know why you don't see that."

"I do." She'd been stroking his hand and slowly she stopped, his hand coming to rest on her breast. He drew down the zipper on her jacket and pulled it off her arms.

Slowly she stripped off her long-sleeved cotton shirt leaving the brown satin bra and her pink pants. "I think I'm in love," he murmured.

A laugh burst from her, then she was quiet again. "I could take it off."

He studied her intensely. From her hair, to the little earrings dangling from her ears, to the sweetheart dip of her neckline, to the grown woman's curve to her breasts and the modest bump of her belly, to her pink pants.

"Take these off."

With the firelight dancing behind her, Melanie pushed the pants down her legs and stepped out of them. The panties and bra matched! He was in love.

The guys at Ryder had hotly debated whether this mattered, and it did. All Rolland knew was that the minute he saw the curve of her hip in panties that matched her bra, he wanted to take them off with his teeth.

She kneeled on the couch reaching for him, and he buried his face in her breasts. The road home seemed to have crossed continents and had brought him back here. He didn't know how, but her bra came away and her breast slid against his tongue, and he'd never tasted skin so sweet. The sounds she made were soft, too, and her hands encouraged him to please her more.

Nothing could have taken him away from her breasts except for the desire to join with her building deep within him.

He held her by her bottom and brought her closer, his tongue sliding between both breasts, his lips bringing her nipples to hardened peaks, wanting all of her in ways he hadn't known before. Her body shook and he held her, unable to let her go.

Rolland stood with her in his arms and she squealed. "What?"

"Be quiet, woman. We're going to bed."

He extinguished the fire and carried her to his room. Rolland stepped out of his remaining clothes before climbing into bed with Melanie.

"The lights don't work, so the nightlights are going to have to do it for a while."

"We'll be asleep soon. The power company will get things together before we wake up tomorrow," Melanie assured him.

She was beneath the flannel sheet, but the outline of her body was so sexy he got harder as he watched his hand move beneath the sheet and stop between her legs.

"You like that?" he asked.

"I do," she exhaled against his cheek.

He penetrated her with his finger, and she rose to meet his thrusts.

He put his head under the covers. When his tongue

touched her, she thought she'd been stroked by a sponge. She was tense having him so close to her most personal parts, but she didn't know how to stop him and frankly, she wanted him there. She'd never experienced oral sex and wanted to know what all the fuss was about. And then he pulled her to him, gently separating the folds, revealing the hidden charm beneath. Every once in a while he'd bite her thigh and she'd follow his mouth where the pleasure took her, but she'd go right back and let his tongue guide her, taking her to a zone so sensual that she could only wonder why she'd never been there before.

Her sensitivity wasn't lost on him as her legs began to tremble when he laved her. Melanie's eyes shot open and she clutched the sheets and a huge sigh burst from her. This feeling scrambling around in her back and bottom and legs needed an outlet. She grabbed his head and pushed him deeper into her, spreading her legs wider. The sensation was like power and source meeting. This was it. This was what women had been keeping secret for centuries. The power gathered in her legs and butt, in her back and hips, and shot up her back and out of her mouth and body in a mind-blowing, body-quaking orgasm.

Melanie hadn't known this was how good making love could be. Her face was wet from crying, but she wasn't done with Rolland. Far from it. She wanted all of him. His hands everywhere. His mouth. His tongue. Him.

"Come here," she said, reaching for him.

"We need condoms," he told her, smiling.

"No," she moaned, her hands seeking him. "I—I can't get pregnant. We tried for seven years. I can't…"

"Mel," he whispered, his sorrow as penetrating as his concern for making an unplanned baby.

She guided his hand to her breasts. His mouth to hers. "It won't happen. Don't worry. Come to me." She reached up to embrace him and kissed his lips, his eyes, his nose. "Please."

He smiled. "You are beautiful."

"More beautiful than Purdy, but not as beautiful as Horace?" she asked, teasing. She drove her hands up his back and over his toned bottom.

Rolland slipped his finger inside of her and she accepted him. "More beautiful than both of them."

She took his sex in her hand, loving the feel of him and how comfortable he seemed with her holding him. His gaze never left hers as he slowly moved back and forth in her hand, his fingers making the same movement inside her. "You ready?" he asked.

Melanie nodded and turned on her side. He kissed her shoulder. "Where are you going?"

"I thought you wanted me to be this way," she said, blushing. "Where do you want me?"

"I want to watch you come this time."

He settled on top of her and she loved the weight of him, had wanted this a very long time. "Oh, Rolland. Don't get your hopes up. It's so soon."

He kissed her until she was silent. "*I'm* in the bed with you. I want to watch you come. Bring your legs up a little."

Melanie did and he sank into her and her eyes rolled back and she smiled. She threw her arms around his neck and kissed him.

"God, you're gorgeous when you smile like that."

He filled her and she sank into the feeling of this beautiful man making love to her. She ran her hands over his skin, needing to touch him like he was touching her, deeply, emotionally, physically. He looked into her eyes and she saw the man in him, the man he was now, the one she'd accepted, the one she wanted, and she leaned up and kissed him, giving him everything she had.

Melanie gasped, her fingers tripping up his ribcage, over his nipples to his throat where his neck muscles strained. He surprised her and snatched her fingers into his mouth and sucked, making her feel even more erotic.

His body pushed against her most intimate parts, so sensitive without protection and when he reached between them and stroked, Melanie could feel the tears coming again. She put her arms around his shoulders wanting him to come close to her.

"No," he said. "I want to see you."

Inching higher the more he pushed inside of her, her toes curled. "It's coming." She put her fingers to her eyes and he slid them to his chest. "Baby, cry if you want to. It's okay."

His thrusts were powerful, his gaze just as intense. She couldn't hold back the emotion any longer. Melanie arched and the tears came as she let go, feeling as if a mini earthquake had rocked the house off its foundation. Her body seemed to consume his, making him come in such a manner that brought him on top of her in a teeth-clenching, body-shuddering finish. When she opened her eyes, they both held the other as if they weren't sure the bed could contain them.

She finally unhooked her legs from his back and he chuckled.

"I'll be right back."

Melanie found the flashlight and hurried into the bathroom. She looked into the mirror after she'd finished and saw her smile, her happiness radiating, and then the caution that replaced it. It stole her smile and gave her a reality check. She was living in a fantasy world. Rolland had a little over a week to go and then his time with Ryder would be done. She needed to help him prepare to leave.

She climbed back into bed and he covered her with the sheet and blanket. "Rolland?"

"Don't ruin this, Mel. This is us. From now on, after Melanie the therapist and Rolland the patient are finished, we're Rolland the man and Melanie the woman."

"Okay."

She was filled with such a sense of relief that ran concurrent with guilt. She didn't sleep a wink.

Chapter Twelve

Melanie nibbled on a pancake from the day before, then threw it into the trash, chiding herself for her bad habits. "I'm getting yogurt when we go into town today." Her stomach felt bloated from eating all the bread Rolland fixed every day for breakfast.

She stood at the counter and stared at her cell phone, her sister's number a thumb-press away. She could call and leave a message. There wasn't any harm in that.

Rolland was still upstairs getting ready for their morning run, but she'd managed to get downstairs for a cup of coffee before the hour of torture began. She'd cut up apples, lemons and oranges and arranged them on a plate before looking at her phone again and imagining their conversation. *Hi, it's me, Mel. Melanie. Your sister. I. I what? How's your family? I just wanted to say hello.* Deborah might forgive her eventually, but Shannon wouldn't. She hadn't been the easily forgiving type. Axel had been so happy to see her a few years ago, but hadn't kept in touch. What would he say now? He had every right to hang up on her and never want to know her again. She exhaled slowly and pressed the button, before putting the phone to her ear.

"What?" an older woman demanded.

"Hello?"

"Who is this?"

"Melanie. I was looking for my sister Deborah Wysh."

"This ain't her number no more, so don't call here again. Do you know what time it is? Six in the morning! Must be out yo' fool mind."

Melanie hung up and the frown held her face frozen. What had she been thinking? Of course it was early, and she was out of her fool mind! She considered calling Shannon and Axel, but she'd already struck out once. That was enough bad news for one day.

Nibbling on an apple wedge, she watched as the neighbors loaded the kids into the car and took off. Maybe tonight she'd get over there and play with Cooper and Lucy.

Suddenly she felt lips on the back of her neck and her knees melted. Those lips had made her soar twice last night and once again this morning. "Besides scaring me," she said, "you have to stop doing that. We had an agreement. After five o'clock." She scooted from beneath his warm hands.

"I want to go shopping today." He took her chastisement in stride and reached for the juice she'd poured and drank, then grabbed some fruit.

"No shopping. We have a schedule to keep."

"You should read your agreement. I've done what you asked me and now you have to do something I asked. Or—" he frowned thinking. "I'm not going to work."

Rolland went to the refrigerator and pulled out a bottled water and drank the entire sixteen ounces without stopping. They hadn't even run yet.

"Rolland, the agreement doesn't say anything about you not doing your work. We're going into the woods today and we're going to try some multiplication now that you've got adding and subtracting down."

He shrugged and walked into the living room and sat on the couch. Melanie stared after him, surprised. "Excuse me, but what are you doing? We can work outside, if you want, but we have a lot of ground to cover. We can skip exercising. That's up to you."

"I want to go shopping. Can you bring the fruit in here?"

Shocked, her head snapped around. He was changing their whole routine. He loved eating in the dining room as much as he loved exercising. She considered not taking the food to him, but didn't know what she'd gain by being equally stubborn. She picked up the plate and walked into the living room. He had on his running clothes, his jacket and his running shoes. Everything seemed in order, but his attitude.

"What's going on?"

"I want to change our routine and go shopping. I want to be in charge of our day and I want to spend my money, and I don't want you to say no. Our time is almost up and I still don't know how to drive and I want to learn and I think this is the perfect day for a lesson. May I have some fruit, please?"

Melanie wondered if this had anything to do with their making love last night and she was almost sorry she'd been unable to resist him. She was losing control and now she was going to have to fight to get it back. "Rolland, it's important for us to stay on task."

"Mel, I've written all my numbers. I've learned the compass. I've traced, colored, repeated, sang and listened to everything you've said. I stay up writing just to prove to you I know my numbers," he said evenly. "I want to do something different today. Can we do that?"

His logic was flawless and his argument...well, logical. Of course he was right, but if she gave in he would be getting his way. She hated the direction of her thoughts and stopped herself. She'd made an agreement and she had to honor it.

"Maybe while we're out today we can talk about where you'd like to live. Maybe we can work together and get two things accomplished at once."

"Maybe. Can I have a kiss?"

"After five," she said firmly. "Come on."

They got up and he took the plate of fruit into the kitchen. "I think you should get another car."

"What's wrong with my car?"

"Lucy is getting a car for her birthday and her windows go up and down if you push a button and yours don't."

She rolled her eyes at him as they got into the car.

"I think you shouldn't have an attitude with me," he told her, as he rolled down his window.

"Quit before you break it. What are we shopping for?"

Melanie pulled onto the highway and merged into traffic. "Pants and a shirt."

"Okay. For anything special?"

"Yes. Something special. That's all I can say."

"All right, then."

Melanie drove him to a men's shop and they headed inside.

"May I help you," a short black man in tan pants and a blue jacket asked.

Rolland looked him up and down. "Mel, I need to talk to him privately about men's business."

"Okay." She put her hands up when the man looked at her skeptically. "He's in charge."

Rolland pulled the man off to the side and then she heard him chuckling. "Okay, sir. I've got you. Come this way, please."

"Mel," Rolland said, "don't follow me. This is for men only."

She nodded. "I know, sweetie. You told me."

He ran back to the tie section where she'd been standing and kissed her on the lips. "Rolland Jones, what are you doing? It's not after five o'clock."

"I decided every time you call me sweetie, I'm kissing you on the lips because it makes me feel good."

She couldn't do anything but put her forehead on his chest. "Finish shopping. I'll be waiting up here for you, sweetie," she whispered.

He kissed her again and was off.

An hour later, when they left the store, Rolland had made friends with the owner and the two salesmen.

Turning out of the plaza, she looked at him. "What's next?"

He pulled out a piece of paper. "Across the street to the mall."

"What are we getting there?"

"Something special for something special."

"Why can't you tell me?"

"Because it's a surprise."

"For whom?"

Rolland shook his head and Melanie sighed. "I don't know why you're being so secretive. I would love to help you," she said.

"You are helping me. You're the driver. Okay, Nordstrom. Okay, Mel. We're here." He patted the dashboard and pointed to a parking space. "Right here. Good. Car in park. Let's go."

"You're very excited." She laughed. He was practically glowing, his fingers tapping happily on his thigh.

"This is fun. Except I'm not driving. But we're going to work on that."

When they got out, Rolland noticed the dark clouds in the sky. He took her hand and they hurried across the parking lot to the mall entrance.

"Winter is coming. I hear it gets really cold down

here. I need to make sure I wash all my sweaters," Melanie commented.

"Where are they?"

"They were in storage, so I've got to dig them out and freshen them up. We've got to get you some."

"Everybody doesn't have winter, do they?"

"Some winters are milder than others. The northern states have cold winters, the midwest generally gets cold and snow, the south gets cold and rain."

Rolland stopped outside of Nordstrom and just stared inside the store.

"Are you okay?"

"This place looks…like it's made for women."

She could feel a grin cover her face. Melanie looped her arms through his. "It's painless. Come on. Where are we going?"

"Second floor. Ladies department."

"What? Why?" They rode the escalator up. "Tell me, Rolland."

"No. It's a surprise. You can't say no. You already promised."

They slid off the escalator and walked to the counter in the ladies department. "I'm Rolland Jones. Cunningham from Bentley's Men's Clothing sent me here with my friend Melanie. We're going to dinner and she needs a nice dress."

"I'm Lara. I'll be glad to help. What's the occasion?"

"Dinner," Rolland told her.

Both women laughed. Melanie caressed his cheek. "You really are quite amazing. But after this we're—"

"Hurry up and find something where I can see your knees and your breasts. I love looking at them."

Lara kept her composure.

Melanie pressed her finger to Rolland's lips, nodded and blinked at him.

"I recognize that look, Mel. I'll sit right over here."

She tried on fifteen dresses before they agreed on a pink knee-length, sleeveless, V-cut dress. He insisted on shoes and jewelry, and by the time they left the mall, darkness had descended. Still, despite the cool evening, Melanie felt feminine and sexy in her dress. A part of her knew Rolland enjoyed all the changing she'd done for him until they'd decided upon this dress.

They stopped at the grocery store and then at Café Amore.

Getting out of the car, Rolland came around and opened her door. "I'm driving home."

"No."

"Okay, then you're teaching me something tomorrow."

"Tomorrow is good," she conceded, unable to hold off any longer. They walked into the café and were engulfed in warmth. "Good evening, Isabel."

"Rolland, Melanie. How are you?" Isabel came from around the counter and greeted them warmly. She wore skinny jeans with pink roses embroidered on them, earrings bearing the same flower swinging from her ears.

"Fine. Why does it get so cold in Kentucky, Isabel, and you stay so cheerful?" Rolland asked her as he took off his coat and hung up Melanie's, too.

"I sell coffee, Rolland." She wiggled her eyebrows.

"I'm happy it's cold. What hot drink can I get you?" She rubbed her hands together and grinned happily.

They both enjoyed their new friend. "Hot chocolate with marshmallows."

Isabel rolled her eyes and shook her head. "Predictable, you two. I'm bringing you cake."

They linked hands over the table and Melanie gazed at Rolland. "We're supposed to be looking at the map and deciding a great place for you to live." She shook his hand, trying to free hers. "I need this, please."

He still held on, his eyes excited. "I've thought it over and I want to live in Georgia."

Her stomach did a somersault. "Really? Why?"

"You lived there. You said it was nice. Not cold like here. Not cold like up north. Hot in the summer. A nice place. There's a big airport in Atlanta and if I don't like it, I can go someplace else. But mostly you live there."

"Rolland, I live here now."

"You aren't staying here forever."

"You don't know that."

He nodded. "You're not attached to this place, Mel. You're like me. Here for a short time, but once you get what you need, you'll go where you're supposed to be."

"Rolland, life isn't that simple. People relocate for jobs all the time and make new lives in new places because of their jobs. That's the way of the world. Don't factor me into your plans. You have to do what's right for you," she said gently.

She dug into her bag and pulled out a piece of paper.

"Now I want to go over the evaluation I'm turning in to Ryder next week. We have a few things that have to be one hundred percent in order for me to sign off."

"Mel, this is Melanie and Rolland adult time. Not therapist and patient time."

"I've done things your way all day and I've got to have a few minutes of work time to say what I've got to say, Rolland, as your therapist."

He smacked the table and she jerked in surprise. Rising, he walked over to the counter and spoke to Isabel. Returning with a pencil, he sat down and on the back of the map wrote the numbers three and four. "Now write eight," she said, controlling her frustration. "Nine. Seven. Six. Two. Ten. Five."

He took his time and she grew more proud with each number he completed. At the end he took the pencil back to Isabel and picked her up in a bear hug. She gave a squeal of delighted surprise. When he got back to the table, Melanie stretched her arms out to him, too.

Rolland scooped her into a kiss so big she didn't know that love could feel so good. They sat down and sipped their hot chocolate.

"You've been practicing," she said quietly as soft jazz filtered through the café speakers.

"After you go to sleep every night. I get up and write. That's the only way I can remember. Then I finally started retaining the numbers and remembering things I'd forgotten like the color of my car. Navy. Crazy things. I have a house with winding stairs."

The door chime tinkled and cold air blew in.

Melanie looked over her shoulder at the new arrivals and squinted in recognition…fear.

"Melanie Wysh, is that you? Is that you, Deion? Oh my goodness, girl. It's been years since I've seen you two. Get up and give me a hug."

Chapter Thirteen

Ivy Curtis was twice as big as Melanie and talked three times as fast. She had a full head of hair and a pretty face. Imposing and commanding, she controlled the room. They'd grown up together in Kentucky and had attended the same college, but later had drifted apart. Melanie had given her a brief explanation for their presence in Kentucky, but Ivy wasn't satisfied.

"You're working here, Melanie?" Her voice banged off the walls. "Why didn't I know this?"

"I just got here a few months ago. It's been an adjustment."

"That's why you call friends. To help you over the rough patches. We were really tight in school. I'm hurt you didn't let me know you were here. I would have called you if I was in Georgia. The last time I saw you, you were living it up in that big fat house in Atlanta. I've always admired the way you lived. So close to the city and cultural events. I still live next door to a chicken farm." Her laugh was as big as the lake behind Scott's beach house.

Rolland smiled when she looked at him.

"But you've always loved living here in Kentucky, right, Ivy?" Melanie said.

"I have. It's simple and quiet, and I love the people. And we do eat our fair share of chicken. So I guess it's right I live next door to the farm."

"Ivy?" Melanie said, but her words had fallen on deaf ears as the woman stared at Rolland.

Rolland had grown accustomed to people staring at him. Before it was because of the scars, but this staring felt different. She was openly curious. Her gaze methodical and assessing.

"You two must be playing a practical joke on me," Ivy mused. "This is Deion or I'm a ballerina."

"Ivy," Mel said firmly, "He isn't Deion! Now, I'm going to have to insist you stop staring. Come on, you're making Rolland uncomfortable." Mel's laugh sounded false. Rolland noticed it, too, over the chime and music, and the talk of the customers. Melanie was lying. For the first time since he'd met her, she looked scared. He'd seen her protective, caring and even desirous, but not afraid or deceitful.

"How's your family, Ivy? I remember your brother had the biggest crush on me. How's he?"

When Ivy dragged her gaze away, it felt as if she'd taken off the top layer of his clothing with her eyes. Rolland watched both women's facial expressions. "Davone's a single father of eight. His wife ran out on him a year ago. He doesn't have time to chase women now, honey. Rolland Jones, is it? Hmm. Must be Deion's twin. They say everybody has one, and I swear to God, you're his. Where is Mr. Wall Street? Remember we used to call Deion that? That man could make money out of air. He's probably somewhere selling windmills. That's the new energy." She laughed to herself.

"We're divorced."

"Can't say I didn't see that coming." She shook her head. "I'm sorry, Melanie."

"That's okay. Ivy, are you still an attorney?" Mel again tried to change the subject and Rolland wondered why. He didn't look at Ivy anymore. Just Melanie.

"No." She adjusted in her seat next to Rolland. "I'm a judge. Circuit court."

Melanie looked like she'd been shocked by an electric current.

"Ma'am, can I get you some cake." Isabel offered, looking uncomfortable, too.

"No thanks, Isabel," Melanie answered before Ivy could accept. "We've got to be going. Rolland's a little under the weather and I need to get him home."

"Mel?" he said. He'd never heard her tell an outright lie before.

"I don't mind leaving," she said, standing. "Come on. Let's go."

Ivy looked between the both of them. "Maybe once my car is fixed tomorrow I can stop by for a visit before heading home. Do you have a local number, Melanie?"

"That sounds—" Rolland said, but Melanie was already shaking her head.

"I don't have the number, and we have plans for tomorrow. I'm taking Rolland into Lexington for a couple of appointments."

"That's far. You sure you can't stay a while longer? I haven't seen you in nearly eight years, girl." Melanie nodded her thanks to Isabel for their coats. She gave her a twenty for their hot chocolates and told her to keep the change.

"We just can't, Ivy. I've got to get him home. It was so good to see you."

"Here, take my number." Her friend looked genuinely hurt. She scribbled on a piece of paper and handed it to Melanie. They hugged quickly and Rolland shook her hand.

"It was nice to meet you."

"Likewise," she said, staring.

Rolland looked at Melanie as Café Amore faded from view behind them. She was driving fast and sped through the red light.

"Mel, what's wrong?"

"Nothing."

"That's the fourth lie you've told tonight. There's nothing wrong with me, you know the number to Scott's house and I don't have any appointments in Lexington tomorrow."

"I know, but there are things I just can't tell you."

"Like why your friend thinks I'm Deion."

They jerked to a stop at the four-way stop and then proceeded more slowly. Rolland didn't miss that her hands were tight on the steering wheel and that her expression was grim.

"Please don't ask me any more questions."

"I deserve answers. I'm confused and I'm not the only one without answers. Ivy is confused, too."

Melanie looked at Rolland and saw her husband Deion. She thought back to the day she'd walked into the gym and when she'd seen Rolland and how she'd felt. She'd known almost immediately that he was her husband. He'd wanted to divorce her. *Had* divorced her. And she'd made a commitment right then that she'd help Rolland Jones learn what he needed to join society, and then she would step back into her life and close the chapter on their past.

Melanie gasped, scared. She hadn't bargained on her love for Rolland growing into this nearly living form that would consume the love she'd once had for him. No, this love was stronger and more vital. Powerful and built on a foundation that was stronger than her selfish want of the past. She'd had to give to him selflessly. All of herself, all the time. Her job required she make him better for the world, but she hadn't counted on becoming a better person as well. Rolland had taught her forgiveness. He'd taught her love in its most delicate sense. She could laugh at the formation of clouds now and she never had before. Rolland had taught her to appreciate the beauty in a raindrop.

The tears she swallowed went down hard. She'd tried to stay impartial, but Rolland hadn't let her. He'd not forgotten one thing, and that demonstrated his determination to live beyond his TBI. That determination was part of his original makeup, yet he was a different man. A beautiful new man. And she was grateful to have known this man. To have been given this second chance at loving her true love.

Now she had to hold her head up and see this little lie through, and take her shattering heart and let him go.

"She doesn't matter. She's just someone from the past that we ran into."

"Mel, she's important, but she's like everyone from your past. You've wiped your past clean. You don't even talk about your family. Have you called your brother and sisters?"

"Yes, and the number has been changed."

"There has to be a way to get another number."

"Rolland, it's not important."

"Yes, it is."

"No, it isn't." She drove onto their street and saw Lucy taking a spin around the cul-de-sac in her shiny new car. They rolled down their windows and waved.

They pulled into their garage and Melanie lowered the door. "Rolland, some things are better left alone, and that's why I'm not discussing my life with you. Don't make me regret our getting close."

She disabled the alarm as Rolland followed her into the house with the bags in his hands.

Melanie stooped to pick up some rose petals that were on the floor. "What's going on here?"

"I'd planned a surprise dinner. That's why I wanted to take us shopping. I thought we could celebrate being nearly finished."

She shook her head. "You shouldn't have. I've let things get too far out of control."

He put the bags on the counter. "You still can't explain why your friend thinks I'm your husband. Where is he? Why don't you call and let me talk to him?"

"You're crazy."

The room seemed to stand still.

"Am I?"

"I didn't mean it that way, Deion—Rolland! Let's just sit down and talk things through."

"You know what, Melanie, up until you called me Deion, I believed everything you said. I've been asking to talk all evening. All week. But now that I'm all tangled up in your lies, I don't want to talk to you anymore."

Rolland took the bags off the counter, walked through the house and upstairs to his room. Melanie followed and stood outside his door.

"I'm sorry, Rolland. I wish you could understand."

"Don't worry about me, Melanie." He changed to jogging pants, a thick long-sleeved top and a hat. He searched his bag for his gloves, but decided to go without them. The run to Café Amore would take at least twenty minutes and he wanted to get there before Ivy left. Leaving his room, he nearly ran over Melanie.

"Where are you going?"

"Running."

"It's dark outside." He bounded down the stairs without replying. "Rolland, it isn't a good idea to run in the dark."

"I live in the dark and you want to keep me there. I'm going to the café to finally get some honest answers." He opened the door and took off.

Chapter Fourteen

His legs moved steadily, demonstrating training and confidence. Rolland was sure of himself, his destination and his purpose.

Melanie was the one who was afraid. She needed for the man she once loved and the man she now loved to never come together. Not this way.

One day he might wake up from this fog and he'd remember who he was, and she didn't want to be there and see the disappointment on his face when he realized he was married to a woman he'd once gotten rid of.

A car horn blared. "Rolland?" Melanie called, pulling up behind him in her car. "Please get in and let's go home."

He stopped to look at the four-way stop sign, then breezed through, while she had to wait her turn. By the time she parked, he was already inside the café. She was at the door when he exited and bumped into her. "Ivy already left," he said, clearly disappointed.

He paced in front of the shop, and Melanie tried to talk to him. "Please come home. I'll tell you as much as I can."

"What's my name?"

"Rolland Jones."

"Not Deion—"

She shook her head. *Not anymore.* "Please come home."

A lady exited the café and he stopped her. "Did you see a heavy-set lady with a black jacket and a purple scarf on leave here?"

"About ten minutes ago."

"Thanks."

She waved and walked on. Melanie rubbed her forehead. "Please let me drive you home. It's cold out here."

"I'm coming back tomorrow for answers, Mel."

"I'll tell you as much as I can, so you won't have to do that." They walked to the car and for the second time that night she drove them home.

When they arrived on the cul-de-sac, the street was quiet. This time Melanie didn't pull into the garage, but parked on the street facing the moon.

"I feel like there's a lot at stake, Melanie. Like something big is about to happen."

"Rolland, your life is changing. You're about to go out on your own. You don't need the people at Ryder anymore. That's why you're feeling this way."

"How don't I need you when I don't know what to do without you? I don't know how to make money or how to do the basic things a man has to in order to support himself. How don't I need you when I love you and you don't love me back? You won't even tell me the truth."

"Rolland, you're going to be okay. You know more than you think you do. You were wonderful today. You wanted to go shopping, and you were a man with a plan. You not only went shopping, but you asked for help and people gave you good information and you used it to get things accomplished. You kept a secret from me. You took me to Nordstrom and bought me clothes and shoes and a purse—" A sob burst out of her and she covered her face. Melanie couldn't stop herself and she leaned over the steering wheel and let the tears come.

"Why are you crying?"

"Rolland, everything is changing and I can't impact your life any further. I have to help you get through this last stage, these last five days and then you're on your own."

"Melanie, you can't let me go. You're the only woman I've felt any real connection to. I have to know what this is. Right now my heart is beating so fast, I'm so scared that you're walking away from me, I don't know what to do. If I'm not Deion, I wish I was. At least then I'd have a past. I'd at least know I was the jerk who treated you like dirt."

"Stop! Don't you say that. He and I are over and I want to at least be your friend forever." Melanie removed the emotion from her voice. "You're going to be fine. We're going to work on giving you tools to help you once you're in the outside world."

She wiped her face and pulled into the garage and they went into the house. She saw the bottles of sparkling cider, the uneaten dinner on the counter and the roses.

She wanted to turn to him, but didn't. "I'm sleeping in my room tonight. Good night."

In her bedroom, Melanie meditated early and felt peaceful with the decision she'd made. She would apologize for her behavior and offer Rolland an explanation about last night. Reading e-mail, her thought process was turned upside down when she saw an article about a patient who'd made a near-full memory recovery.

His family was elated.

She leaned back and closed her eyes. That would alter the course of many lives if that happened to her. She had to stop interfering. The ringing phone disrupted her near-sleep. "Hello?"

"Is this Melanie Bishop?"

"Um, Melanie Wysh, but yes. Who is this?"

"You're back to using your family name. Why?"

"Deborah?" Melanie forced herself into full consciousness, thankful for the forgiving sound of her sister's voice.

"Yes, it's me. My client has Alzheimer's and sometimes she gets my phone when my back is turned. I'm sure sorry I missed your call."

"Deborah, it's so good of you to call me back."

"I figured you'd come around sooner or later. Axel's on the line, and so is Shannon."

Melanie's hand flew to her chest. "Hi, Axel. Hi, Shannon." Melanie heard herself and she knew she sounded like a little girl.

"Hey, Mel," Axel said. "It's sure good to hear your voice again. How have you been?"

"I've been okay."

"Not so good if you're a Wysh again," Shannon said.

Melanie folded her legs beneath her and a tear slapped her ankle. She massaged it into her skin. "Well, Bacon, I knew I'd hear the truth from you and to be honest, my life has taken several turns. Deion and I are divorced. I live in Kentucky, and I work at the Ryder Rehabilitation Center." Melanie paused a moment, then continued. "I shouldn't have walked away from you all. That was wrong. I was young and stupid and I called because one of my patients doesn't have anyone and I—"

"You have me," Deborah said imploringly. "Everybody makes mistakes. Just don't do it again."

"I won't," she whispered.

"When I saw you a few years ago, I knew that wasn't you walking away from me. It was him. I couldn't understand that, Melanie," Axel told her. "But when you were little, you were always the one to make me laugh about something. I'm willing to give you another chance."

"Thanks, Axel."

"I'll have to think about it," Shannon said coldly. "We needed you these past years. People have been sick. Family has died and gone through hard times. This isn't about money, but about being a family, Melanie. While you were sitting down there playing rich girl, we were up here in Richmond slaving to save Momma and Daddy's house and farm."

"You calling her 'rich girl,' means it is about money to you, Shannon. We've made it through," Deborah said sternly. "She was twenty-four when this started. At the same age, you were having your third baby, and as I recall, not contributing much either. So that's quite enough."

"But you never looked back, did you, Melanie?"

"I thought of you all often, Shannon. I'm not proud of myself. I was hoping to make amends."

"Well, you can start by paying your share of the property taxes."

Melanie heard the challenge now the way Deion had heard the pleas for money then. Too much and too often.

"I borrowed seventy-five hundred dollars from Melanie and Deion and never paid them back," Axel said. "I can see why Mel would never want to be bothered with us. She hasn't been on the phone for ten minutes and she's getting shaken down. Shannon, look at it like this—for seven years I paid her taxes. Okay?"

Melanie's thumb shook uncontrollably over the End button where it had hovered, but after her brother had spoken, she rested her hand on her thigh. "Thank you, Axel."

"I didn't borrow as much, but I did, too," Deborah said. "I meant to pay it back, but I kept putting you off until I just didn't hear from you anymore. Then I got angry, like you two didn't have the right to be angry, and then I was insulted. We were family. And now I'm ashamed."

"Deb, don't be. I shouldn't have disappeared. It wasn't

ever about the money. Maybe it was for Deion, but he never said that to me. He just got quiet and that was it."

"Sometimes that's how men are."

"I'm really sorry I wasn't there for you all. I really am."

"You don't have to keep apologizing," Axel said. "Like Deb said, we're all guilty of one thing or another at one time or another. So I'm letting bygones be bygones.

"You don't live in Georgia at all?" Axel wanted to know.

"No. I live here in Kentucky."

"Where do you live here?" Axel asked.

"Springleaf."

"You're only a few hours from home."

"I know, but I'm living in a home with a patient and can't get away until he's finished with his treatment. We won't be finished for another week."

"Where's Deion?" Deborah asked.

"He was in a terrible accident and well, he suffered irreparable brain injury."

Her sisters gasped and Axel moaned. "I'm sorry, Melanie. Was this before your divorce?" Axel wondered. He'd always been a compassionate person. Never hurt anyone in his life.

"About the same time."

"Mel, you sound like you need family right now," Deborah said.

Tears clogged her throat and for a few seconds she couldn't speak. "No, you know. Shannon is right. I made this bed, I'm going to see this through. I'd better go. I've got to get started on the day."

The house alarm beeped signaling that it had been disengaged. Melanie heard Rolland's voice, and then a knock on her door.

"Come in."

"Good morning," he said, holding Cooper.

"Good morning, Rolland. You sleep well?" She assessed him and dismissed their difficult evening. She didn't want to fight or disagree.

"Yes." He was cradling the baby so lovingly, her heart swelled.

"Looks like we've got company. Hey, Cooper. How are you? What's going on next door?" Melanie was up and took the baby who made little sucking sounds. Rolland looked into her eyes as if he'd missed her.

"Todd and Jacquie wanted to know if we'd watch Cooper while they took Lucy and Chase to the doctor. She's got popcorn stuck up her nose and Chase has the flu."

"That little girl is a mess. Of course we'll babysit. Did you tell them? They must have just pulled off."

"Yes. Are you on the phone?" he asked. She still had it in her hand as she cradled Cooper.

"Oh my goodness, yes! Hello?" Melanie grappled the phone to her ear.

"Melanie?" Deborah said. "He sounds like Deion."

"I know, Deb."

"Oh my God. It's him. He doesn't know you're you?"

"No, ma'am." She turned away and dabbed her tears into Cooper's blanket. The baby woke for a second and smiled at her. "Rolland, are you hungry?" she asked as he looked on the dresser at her perfume bottles.

"I can make pancakes," he offered excitedly.

She laughed a little. "I think I'm too fat for pancakes today. How about yogurt and fruit?"

"Mel, you're too skinny. I think you need some bread. We'll have meat sandwiches."

Axel chuckled. "That's definitely not Deion. Mel, you sure you don't need us there today? How are you going to handle half a man and a baby?"

"We'll manage. We're going to babysit and get to work. Thanks for calling me back. Please call again. Anytime," she added.

"You say you have a house there," Deb asked.

"Yes."

"Give me the address right now."

Mel rattled it off and gently rocked Cooper in her arms.

"We love you, Melanie."

"I love you, too," she said to Deborah, but she was talking to all of them.

She heard Axel's voice, but not Shannon's. That was okay. Rome wasn't built in a day.

The rain turned to thundershowers, and Melanie made tea. They ate their dinner from the night before for lunch and settled down to an easy day of work.

"You and Ivy went to Georgia State together?"

Melanie nodded, surprised he'd remember such a thing. "I studied psychology and she studied pre-law. She then attended Emory's law school, and look at her now."

"Where did Deion come into the picture?"

She hesitated, then answered carefully. "We met my

senior year. I thought we were right for each other, but we were too different. I know that now."

Rolland lay on a blanket on the floor, Cooper lying next to him. Rolland looked up at papers she held over her head and read the words on them. "So if I'm not Deion, why wouldn't I be perfect for you? Clown. Train. Cat. Shoe. Dog. Why aren't I perfect?"

"You've been in a controlled environment and you don't know what's out there. You might get back to Vegas and discover you love it there."

He shook his head. "I watched a movie about it on TV and I don't like it. Basketball. Football. Mel, stop with the papers. I know all of those words. What are you going to do without me? You're going to be lonely. I take good care of you, you know."

Melanie looked at Rolland and Cooper and didn't know how to respond.

Everything she wanted was in that room, but wasn't hers. She couldn't interfere anymore with the course of Rolland's life.

"I'm going back to Ryder and work with more patients. The rest of this week we're going to work on cooking and your absolute favorite thing... driving."

"You're serious?" His eyes lit up like Christmas lights on a tree.

She nodded. "You've exceeded all my expectations."

He carefully crawled around the baby, but she held up her hands. "We can't kiss. I can't. Not anymore."

"Why, Mel? My heart wants you. My body wants you.

This is love, Melanie. I believe it is. I don't have anything to judge it against, but that's what I believe it is."

He touched his face to her neck and she felt flushed. "Rolland, you have to understand, we're in this closed-off environment and it's easy for both of us to think we have certain feelings. But once our worlds go back to normal, those feelings will change, too."

"This is normal to me, Mel. This happy feeling inside of me is good. I don't want it to go away."

She nodded, understanding. "I wish I could change the circumstances, but I have to do what's right for you."

"What about you?"

"I've been wrong in this entire situation and I'm going to pay for it. Trust me. Now let's watch TV or cook something."

Rolland didn't say anything as she crawled over and talked to Cooper who lay on the blanket watching them talk the entire time. He kicked his feet now that she was talking to him and smiled, passing gas.

"He probably needs a different kind of formula," she said offhandedly.

"I vote for cooking," Rolland said. "Are you hungry for dinner?"

"Not really. Did Todd and Jacquie say when they'd be back?"

Rolland shook his head. Cooper whimpered and Melanie put her hand on his stomach and rocked him. "What's up, little baby?"

"He drank all of his milk." Rolland went to the kitchen for his diaper bag and looked inside.

Melanie looked up. "He did? I thought there were more bottles?"

He shook his head. "They were empty. There's a can of powder in here and that's all."

Melanie got up, talking to the baby. "Cooper, I don't think you've ever been in my kitchen before. We've got Uncle Rolland working very hard to make you a bottle."

She carried him around and he was making noises, happy to be up and about.

"Mel, I can't do that."

Cooper cried a little and Melanie patted his back, talking to him. "Uncle Rolland is going to make you a nice bottle and we're going to watch. Read the back of the can, Rolland, and follow the instructions."

"You trust me to do this?" he asked, the can in his hand.

"Yes." She rubbed his arm to reassure him. "We trust you."

Rolland measured, poured and shook the formula in a lidded cup before actually pouring it into the baby's bottle. He handed Melanie the bottle, his expression triumphant.

"Thank you," she said and sat down with Cooper on the sofa.

Rolland stayed in the kitchen and then joined her and the baby. "Remember I told you I thought I had a family with eight kids?"

She nodded, watching Cooper's sleepy eyes. Turning, she looked at Rolland and realized her mistake. His gaze was upon her, and then it dawned on her. She loved him completely. She simply could not tell him their past relationship. When and if his memory returned, he would be angry that he'd been duped by the woman he'd divorced. She'd be hurt all over again. But much worse for having fallen in love with him twice.

"Yes?"

"I don't feel that way anymore."

"I'm sorry, Rolland."

"I want to be with you again."

Cooper stopped sucking and sighed. They both laughed as if the subject bored him silly.

She shook her head and Rolland kissed her neck. "You have to stop. You're going to make this difficult for both of us."

"I want you to have a Cooper for me. For us."

Melanie captured his jaw in her hand. "Don't break my heart, Rolland."

"That's the way I feel when you keep telling me no." He put his forehead to hers and just sat beside her and let the night surround them.

About twenty minutes later, there was a knock at the door and Melanie awakened and got off the floor in the living room where the three of them had lain down. Todd stood outside with an umbrella and an apology.

"Come in. Is everything okay?"

"No. Chase has the flu and the doctor wanted to keep him overnight, so we had to drive over to the hospital."

Melanie touched his arm. "I'm so sorry I wasn't downstairs today when you came by. Cooper is fine. You could have left him until tomorrow."

"We didn't want to trouble you. My mom is here

now, anyway." He tiptoed inside. "No signs of a temperature or anything?"

She shook her head. "None. He was quite happy. We stayed down here so we would hear you when you got back. Here, let me get his things together. How's Lucy?"

Todd touched his forehead. "In the hospital, too. There weren't just popcorn kernels in her nose. She'd put a magnet in there, too. Luckily just one. Right now, they're working it through her body."

"Are you serious?" Melanie gave him the diaper bag and then gingerly picked up the baby.

Todd nodded. "My mother blames me and Jacquie for not watching the kids more closely." His eyebrows shot up and Melanie gave him a sympathetic pat on the back. "She's going to try to steal Cooper, I know she is.

"How's Rolland been?"

She gazed at him lovingly. "Good." She nodded. "Good."

"If you look at him like that, then he's better than good."

"Todd, every therapist has a special patient."

"That look tells me he's more than a patient to you. We should be home tomorrow. Stop by, okay?"

She nodded. "Good night and if you need anything, we're here."

Melanie watched them go and turned off the lights. The solar night lights were still on around the room, and she made her way back to the pallet they'd made for the baby and themselves.

"Rolland, it's time to go to bed."

He didn't move, sound asleep, his head on a couch

cushion, his back against the couch. Melanie considered getting down there with him, but they'd end up making love and she couldn't do that again. She had to stay true to what little convictions she had left. Melanie climbed onto the couch and pulled a blanket over herself. She made sure Rolland was covered up and went to sleep.

Chapter Fifteen

The knock was startling and Rolland wasn't sure where it was coming from. Sitting up, he looked around and saw that he was in the living room sleeping on the floor and that Melanie was asleep on the couch. Cooper was gone. He searched under the covers for the baby, but couldn't find him. Knocking shook the door again.

"Melanie, where's the baby?"

He hurried to the door and opened it. The alarm buzzed and he stared at the police officers unsure why they were there. "We're looking for the baby now. Melanie, where's the baby?"

"No," he heard her say then she hurried past him and turned off the alarm. "Cooper is fine. He's at home. What's going on?"

"Deion Bishop?" The officers stepped into the house and Melanie put her hands between him and the officers.

"I think I am. People keep telling me I am. Melanie, tell me the truth."

Rolland stared at Melanie and she nodded. "What is this about?"

"Put your hands behind your back, please."

Rolland did as he was told, but wasn't sure why. "What's happening?"

"You're under arrest."

The officer began to read him his rights and Rolland couldn't comprehend what was happening, only that Melanie was scared and what he saw on her face wasn't half as bad as what he was feeling inside.

The shorter of the two officers shook his head. "It's a good cover faking a brain injury to cover your crimes in Georgia, but not good enough. You're coming with us."

"He's not faking anything. He's Rolland Jones. That's the name that was given to him in the hospital in Las Vegas where he was treated after his accident. Do not hurt him. He's a patient at Ryder Rehabilitation Center. I'm his therapist."

The officer looked at the cozy living room setting, the covers on the floor and then back at them.

"She slept on the couch. I slept on the floor with the baby."

The officer led Rolland from the house. "We'll let Georgia decide who he really is. They say he's Deion Bishop."

"Let me get my purse. I'll come with you."

The tall officer blocked the doorway looking down at her. "You can't do anything for him, Miss."

Panicked, Melanie ran for the phone, slipped and fell. The officer turned around and helped her up. "Miss, slow down. He's going to be okay."

"Don't hurt him. He hasn't done anything wrong. What are the charges?"

"Insider trading and securities fraud."

"What's going to happen?"

"He faces an arraignment, bond hearing and then extradition."

"I need to be with him."

"That's not likely if you're not a doctor or attorney. The best thing you can do is get him an attorney."

Melanie limped around looking for her purse, rubbing her knee.

As soon as the squad cars left, Todd was in the house and Melanie held on to the counter and tried to get to her cell phone.

"Melanie, what's going on?"

She tried not to cry, but couldn't hold herself together any longer. Hot tears slid off her face. "They arrested him for insider trading in Georgia. Securities fraud. What is that?"

"Using insider stock information before the public has the knowledge. That's not our guy. And if it was, it's not him now."

She sobbed and Jacquie patted her back. "Honey, you have to get hold of yourself. First, Todd, hold Cooper while I see about her knee."

"I'm okay. I just want to go down to the station, but they said I can't do anything."

"You can't."

"Not even if I'm his wife?"

"What?" they said, shocked.

"Wait," Jacquie said. "Let's sit down." They helped her into the living room and onto the couch. "Now, what's this about you two being married?"

"We were married for seven years before he had his accident and he divorced me. I am actually Rolland's ex-wife. I didn't know about his accident when I got the job at Ryder. I came here and was introduced to him as Rolland, my patient. He doesn't know me, he doesn't know about our former life and he doesn't know that I love him. I've kept it that way so he can go on with his life. So that he can have a future."

"Melanie, you have to know he loves you," Todd said. "That's all he talked about during our time together."

"I'm aware of that, but in my experience, he might get his memory back and when and if he does, who will he be angry at for being remarried to the woman he wanted to be divorced from, himself or me?"

"Oh my goodness. You poor thing," Jacquie said. "She's right. I felt as if you two were a couple," Jacquie went on. "I feel as if he really loves you."

Melanie shook her head. "He loves the idea of me. He's been in a controlled environment since the accident and it's natural to feel a closeness to those who take care of you."

"But you know it's more than that, right?" Todd said, handing them healthy drinks, sitting down.

Melanie nodded.

"It might help if you start from the beginning and tell us everything. Hold on. Let me get Scott in on this, too." Todd patched Scott in.

Melanie told them everything, editing the parts about their lovemaking, but not about their falling in love again.

"Why did the police come to the house this morning?" Scott sounded baffled and angry.

"They said they'd received a call from someone named Cali who'd informed them that she'd just confirmed the ID of a patient from Las Vegas, one Deion Bishop going under the alias Rolland Jones. She'd seen Deion's picture on TV and realized he and Rolland were the same person. Further checking confirmed that the two are one and the same. It also connected Deion to the warrant for his arrest on insider trading and securities fraud."

Everyone listened quietly until she was finished.

"I'm sorry to have to do this, but I'm suspending you, Melanie. You put Ryder at great risk."

"Scott, I didn't. We're divorced, and Rolland's received excellent care. He's ready to return to society with controls in place. No, he can't drive, but neither can a lot of our patients. And I didn't know about the fraud or insider trading."

"I still have to suspend you. I have to do damage control. You'll be paid for the time your situation is under investigation."

"That's not the point. Why isn't Cali being suspended? Who allowed her to release private information about patients?"

"Melanie, the reputation of the company is at stake. Let me handle all of the important points you've just raised. Meanwhile, Todd is an attorney and can help with getting Rolland out of jail."

Melanie stared up at the neighbor she hadn't known was anything more than a nice man. He patted her knee and winked at her.

"I'll take care of it. And I expect that there's going to be a full investigation. I don't know what kind of man Rolland was before, but he's a great man now, Scott. I'll testify to that."

"I believe all of you. Melanie, I want you to go home."

"To Georgia? I can't. I have a house here in Kentucky. I'll go there."

"Melanie, this is going to blow up in our faces. Go back to Georgia and wait for word from me. You need to move quickly so that you can outrun the media."

"I'm not going back to Georgia. I don't have a house there. The house that's there is Deion's. I'm going back to my house here in Kentucky."

"Okay. She's made up her mind," Jacquie said, brokering no more discussion. "I'll take care of closing up this house."

"Will you tell him where I am?"

"If Scott and Todd don't I will," Jacquie said firmly.

"I'm glad that's covered," Scott said. "Now everyone knows what they have to do. Let's move quickly."

Chapter Sixteen

Rolland sat in his lawyer's office and listened to the charges that had been brought against him and wished he understood them. He was accused of trading on non-public information and making millions of dollars of commissions for the firm where he worked.

Floyd Crooker, the attorney who had been hired by Melanie with Todd's advice, sat beside him and offered advice that involved fighting it out in court or a plea bargain. He could go to jail.

Rolland wished he could remember what happened.

"What if I take the plea?"

"You'll do jail time."

"Why?"

Floyd looked frustrated. That was one thing Rolland had learned since leaving Ryder. People in the outside world were impatient and disbelieving souls. If a person wasn't like them, they were disposable. Although he'd suffered an injury, no one could see it. Therefore it didn't exist. His attorney had probably given him this answer before, but Rolland didn't remember.

"The courts aren't sympathetic to rich executives who use the inside advantage to pad their coffers—to their own benefit, Rolland. You'll get ten years at least."

A knock sounded on the door and they both looked up.

"Come in."

Rolland stood and extended his hand to Cornelius Bunt, an investigator he'd hired. "I've got good news."

All three sat down. "Let's hear it," Floyd said.

"You were in Vegas for a meeting with investor Imelda DeMorrio. She wanted to invest one million dollars in the market and at the same time you were ready to break from your firm. You were scouting her."

"I was. What's scouting?"

"You wanted to take her with you to your own firm."

"What did I do?"

"You went to meet with her and some of her friends to get them to invest with your new firm. Prior to that they'd wanted to see what you could do, and Imelda had put you to a test of sorts."

Rolland sat forward. "A test? How do you test someone in the stock market? You study the stocks over time, watch the trends and know the business and then make a recommendation."

Cornelius nodded. "You've got it. Well, Imelda gave you five stocks to choose from and you had one hour to make a recommendation as to your best choice."

"That's ridiculous." Rolland sat down, his heart beating hard. "I feel ridiculous listening to this. I went for that?"

Cornelius smiled. "You were a ballsy guy. This is what happened. You chose Snoillim."

Rolland lifted his hands. "I'm in trouble about that now."

"I know. But Imelda recorded the interview on DVD." Cornelius shook his head. "She tapes everything. Rolland, you read newspaper stock reports and showed them how to choose stocks. You talked about reading company reports and then you told them 'your best guess.' You didn't have insider info—it's clear from the DVD that was the first time you'd analyzed the stock. It turns out that Imelda acted on your advice and placed an order with your firm when she couldn't find you. When the stock shot up and you went missing, the D.A. thought it was insider trading and issued a warrant."

"My best guess? I said that?"

Cornelius nodded. "I have it all on DVD. No judge in the world will convict you with this evidence."

Floyd jumped out of his seat. "You're kidding?"

"Was Rod Burke aware of this?" Rolland asked.

"I don't believe so. Not of the interview. You weren't working for him. You'd already quit and were trying to establish yourself."

"Floyd, with this evidence, what will happen?" Rolland wanted to know.

"The D.A. will likely want to interview Ms. DeMorrio and the others further, and I'll push for a dismissal."

Rolland stood and got his coat.

"Where are you going?" Floyd asked him.

"Home. Cornelius, I need you to find my house."

The man smiled. "Come on. I think I might know where that is already."

He shook Floyd's hand and walked out.

The front door swung on its hinges, and Rolland smiled as he watched it open, thinking it was rather cool inside.

A Hispanic woman and man approached. "Mr. Deion! Oh heavenly Father, you have answered our prayers! You are back! Melanie said you might not ever come back, and you are here."

Rolland extended his hand to the woman who ran for him. He naturally opened his arms and embraced her.

"And I'm Jusef, Juanita's husband." The men shook hands.

"Rolland, well. Deion. Call me Rolland."

"We heard all about you on the news," Juanita said, looking up at him, her hand in his. "Come on and sit down in the living room. We were just cleaning."

"Do you live here now?" Rolland asked.

The couple laughed. "No. We're cleaning up for you. For a whole year Melanie paid in advance in case you came back. We've been staying this week hoping you would come so we could talk to you. I knew you were going to come back, didn't I say Jusef? I knew. When Melanie left, she cried so much. She was sick. Crying on the floor right there. I came over here and picked her up and we prayed for her. Her hair was so long and pretty and she hadn't combed it. She was so sad."

"She was crying?" A tear slid from his eye. "I shouldn't have hurt her like that."

"You didn't mean to. She left all this furniture for you and she gave us the beds. And she left you this house."

Rolland looked around. "I don't want it. She didn't like it here."

Juanita looked him in the eye. "She just wanted you and babies. That's all."

Jusef left and came back into the living room and handed Rolland an envelope. "Melanie asked me to mail this and I never got around to it. I was hoping to talk to you about it in person one day and I guess this is the day. After you read these, you can tell me if you want me to follow through and mail them."

Juanita went and stood beside her husband. Rolland pulled the papers from the envelope and read them. "They're divorce papers."

"That's right. But they're not legal until they're filed with the courts. If you tear them up, they're not good anymore. Or I can mail them, if you want me to."

He'd felt hopeless and now there was hope.

Rolland went over and embraced Jusef and kissed Juanita on the cheek. "No, thank you. I would like to tear these up right now. And then I'd like to go find my wife."

Melanie answered her door and was swept into her sister Deborah's arms.

Her whole body cried. She didn't know what else to

do. Her name and face had been all over the news and she and Rolland's story had been categorized as being the greatest love story. And the most tragic.

He'd left Kentucky weeks ago and she hadn't heard from him. She'd been fired from Ryder and nobody in the country would hire her.

All she could do was cry into her sister's shoulder. "Come on now, Paddle," Deborah said, using her childhood nickname. "You've got to pull yourself together. You're going to make yourself sick. And we can't have that. You have to keep up your strength."

Deborah had taken the height in the family at five-nine and she was a big woman. She practically carried Melanie to the sofa and put her down.

"He hasn't come for me, Deb. He's really gone. I can't do this again. I love him so much. I hurt so much."

"I know. I'm sorry, Melanie."

Melanie hugged the pillow and couldn't see through her tears. Her sister covered her with the chenille blanket Jacquie had given her and looked worried.

Melanie sat up, her body encumbered by grief. She'd been strong for weeks, but today had taken its toll. The news had shown reports of Rolland in front of their former home with a woman. Just the thought of him with someone else had sent her over the edge.

"But at least there was new evidence that may clear him, according to the story."

Deborah stroked her back. "I want you to come and stay with me. I'll take care of you, and you can help me, too. I never knew owning an assisted living center would be so tough. There's all types of things you can do."

Melanie dried her eyes. It was time to move on. She nodded and her sister sighed in relief. "Okay, Deb. Okay. I'll come. Maybe in a year I'll be able to get a job and start over."

"Honey, there's no rush," Deborah told her. "Besides, you have grounds for a wrongful termination suit against Ryder. At least they fired Cali, although that's no consolation to you."

Melanie shook her head. "I should have disclosed my relationship with him from the beginning. What I did was unethical. I'm lucky to still have my license. Thanks to Todd and Jacquie, and you. I just wanted to help him. I still love him." She took the tissue her sister offered and dried her tears.

"Honey, they saw that," Deborah said.

Melanie put her hands to her face. "No more tears."

Deborah nodded. "I'll pack your clothes. Is there anything else you want to take with you?"

Melanie looked around the home she'd made and swallowed the lump in her throat, shaking her head. "No. Just the clothes and toiletries. Can we leave tonight?"

A look of relief passed over her sister's face. She nodded. "Of course."

Melanie heard her sister talking on the phone in the bedroom, discussing her situation and the fragility of her mental state, but she didn't care to chime in. She knew she'd be okay, but she was heartbroken and she didn't know how to recover faster than to head straight through the pain and come out on the other side.

Now that she'd vowed to stop crying, she felt a

little better, and she reached for another tissue and cleaned her face.

A knock sounded at the door and she got up, but she heard Deborah coming from the bedroom. "I got it. You rest. Oh my," she said, startled. "I'm going in the back and closing the door."

Melanie smelled the roses before she saw them and tasted the chocolate before she actually tasted it.

Being pregnant did that to her.

She sat up and looked over her shoulder. "Rolland, you're here. I didn't think—" She exhaled.

"You knew I would come. I hope you knew."

"I wanted to, but I got scared." Her eyes grew glassy again and she got off the couch. "Are those for me?"

Rolland looked so good and so serious. "Yes, these are for you."

His hands were full and she went to him and took the flowers and candy and the bag hanging off his arm and put them on the table behind the sofa. He had on a thick winter coat with a long zipper and looped buttons and Melanie undid each one before unzipping him. She didn't even let him get his coat off, she just reached inside, wrapped her arms around him and hugged him.

"I missed you. I love you," he said repeatedly. "I love you."

He held her and kept telling her until her rocking ended. His lips found hers. This was where he was supposed to be.

Rolland looked around the living room and saw their lives captured in photographs on every wall. He slid out of his coat and took her hand. "Tell me about us."

She grabbed more tissue, unwilling to let his hand go. "We met at Georgia State, you were twenty-one and I was twenty. We had big dreams. My brother and sisters dubbed you Mr. Wall Street and they always called me Paddle because I was known to get into trouble and get the paddle."

He rubbed her bottom and she slid her arm around his waist and left it there.

"You started working after graduation. This is our wedding picture. We got married when I was twenty-four and you were twenty-five."

"You told me we tried to have a baby, but we never did?" He picked up photographs and looked at them. "You're never smiling."

She shook her head. "I was happy, but my sister had three kids and I didn't have any. We made good money, but the one thing I wanted we couldn't have. You worked late more and more and we grew distant."

"Who is this? This is my mother," he guessed and Melanie nodded.

"That's right. She had you late in life and she's in a nursing home now. I still pay her bills every month."

He caught her in a big hug. "You're a good woman and I'll never forget that again."

"I believe you."

"Why didn't you tell me who I was, Mel?"

"I didn't want to lose you again," she cried, and he captured her in an embrace so loving, she knew love had never been so good.

"I'm never leaving you again. I love you. Tell me about us."

They moved around the room to the later years, looking at photos of them at their summer place and on exotic vacations. "I'm sorry I can't remember these vacations. You look hot! And I mean sexy."

She laughed and her body seemed to rejoice as her depression lifted. "Thank you."

"That's our old house."

"Your house," she corrected.

"No, I'm selling it."

Melanie eyed him curiously. "How did you sell that house? I just saw you on TV in front of it with a woman and you were smiling."

"That was my Realtor."

Melanie burst out laughing. "You're kidding?"

"No. I have even better news. It looks like all the charges are going to be dropped against me."

Melanie took him back to the couch and sat down. "All of them?"

He nodded. "All of them. We'll be free from all restrictions and ethics and rules. We can be in love, if that's what we want to be."

She held him as tightly as he held her. "It's more than what I want to be. I'm already in love with you," she said, trying not to cry.

"Are you trying not to cry again?"

She nodded. "Yes. I promised my family I'd stop. I love you so much and I didn't think you were going to come back for me. I cried every day."

Rolland rubbed her back and finally kissed her. "I

was coming back even if I had to go to every house in this state and find you."

She looked into his eyes. "Rolland, will you marry me?"

He pulled her into his lap and chuckled, kissing her cheek. "No. You are already spoken for."

"What?"

He reached into the bag that he'd brought inside and pulled out the divorce papers he'd ripped in half.

Melanie was puzzled. "This is our divorce decree. Jusef never mailed it. He wanted to talk to me about it first and see if I wanted to change my mind. Because it hasn't been filed, it isn't legal."

Pure happiness rushed over her. "I think you should toss it into the fireplace."

"Great idea."

Rolland got up and put the papers inside and they started to burn. Melanie linked hands with him and watched as the paper was consumed. "Are you going to be happy being Deion Bishop again?"

He shook his head no. "I don't know him. I'd like to change my name, but I thought we'd talk about it."

"I think Rolland Jones is the perfect name for a new father. I think the sooner we make that legal, the better."

"A father?" He captured her in a soul-stirring kiss. "I'm the happiest man in the world. I love you, Melanie."

"I love you, too. Forever."

* * * * *

We'll be spotlighting a different series
every month throughout 2009
to celebrate our 60th anniversary.

Look for Silhouette® Nocturne™ in October!

Travel through time to experience tales
that reach the boundaries of life and death.
Bestselling authors Lindsay McKenna, Cindy
Dees, P.C. Cast and Merline Lovelace join
together in a brand-new, four-book
Time Raiders miniseries.

TIME RAIDERS

August—*The Seeker*
by *USA TODAY* bestselling author Lindsay McKenna

September—*The Slayer* by Cindy Dees

October—*The Avenger*
by *New York Times* bestselling author and
coauthor of the House of Night novels P.C. Cast

November—*The Protector*
by *USA TODAY* bestselling author Merline Lovelace

Available wherever books are sold.

nocturne™

New York Times **bestselling author
and co-author of the House of Night novels**

P.C. CAST

**makes her stellar debut
in Silhouette® Nocturne™**

THE AVENGER

Available October wherever books are sold.

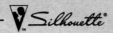

SPECIAL EDITION

FROM *NEW YORK TIMES*
BESTSELLING AUTHOR

SUSAN MALLERY

DESERT ROGUES

THE SHEIK AND THE BOUGHT BRIDE

Victoria McCallan works in Prince Kateb's palace.
When Victoria's gambling father is caught cheating
at cards with the prince, Victoria saves her father from
going to jail by being Kateb's mistress for six months.
But the darkly handsome desert sheik isn't as harsh as
Victoria thinks he is, and Kateb finds himself attracted to
his new mistress. But Kateb has already loved and lost
once—is he willing to give love another try?

Available in October wherever books are sold.

Visit Silhouette Books at www.eHarlequin.com

SSE65481

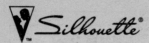

Silhouette®

Romantic
SUSPENSE

Sparked by Danger, Fueled by Passion.

The Agent's Secret Baby

by *USA TODAY* bestselling author
Marie Ferrarella

TOP SECRET DELIVERIES

Dr. Eve Walters suddenly finds herself pregnant
after a regrettable one-night stand and turns to an
online chat room for support. She eventually learns
the true identity of her one-night stand: a DEA agent
with a deadly secret. Adam Serrano does not want
this baby or a relationship, but can fear for Eve's
and the baby's lives convince him that this is what
he has been searching for after all?

Available October wherever books are sold.

Look for upcoming titles in
the TOP SECRET DELIVERIES miniseries
The Cowboy's Secret Twins by Carla Cassidy—November
The Soldier's Secret Daughter by Cindy Dees—December

Visit Silhouette Books at www.eHarlequin.com

REQUEST YOUR FREE BOOKS!

2 FREE NOVELS PLUS 2 FREE GIFTS!

SPECIAL EDITION®

Life, Love and Family!

YES! Please send me 2 FREE Silhouette Special Edition® novels and my 2 FREE gifts (gifts are worth about $10). After receiving them, if I don't wish to receive any more books, I can return the shipping statement marked "cancel." If I don't cancel, I will receive 6 brand-new novels every month and be billed just $4.24 per book in the U.S. or $4.99 per book in Canada. That's a savings of at least 15% off the cover price! It's quite a bargain! Shipping and handling is just 50¢ per book.* I understand that accepting the 2 free books and gifts places me under no obligation to buy anything. I can always return a shipment and cancel at any time. Even if I never buy another book from Silhouette, the two free books and gifts are mine to keep forever.

235 SDN EYN4 335 SDN EYPG

Name	(PLEASE PRINT)	
Address		Apt. #
City	State/Prov.	Zip/Postal Code

Signature (if under 18, a parent or guardian must sign)

Mail to the **Silhouette Reader Service:**
IN U.S.A.: P.O. Box 1867, Buffalo, NY 14240-1867
IN CANADA: P.O. Box 609, Fort Erie, Ontario L2A 5X3

Not valid to current subscribers of Silhouette Special Edition books.

Want to try two free books from another line?
Call 1-800-873-8635 or visit www.morefreebooks.com.

* Terms and prices subject to change without notice. Prices do not include applicable taxes. Sales tax applicable in N.Y. Canadian residents will be charged applicable provincial taxes and GST. Offer not valid in Quebec. This offer is limited to one order per household. All orders subject to approval. Credit or debit balances in a customer's account(s) may be offset by any other outstanding balance owed by or to the customer. Please allow 4 to 6 weeks for delivery. Offer available while quantities last.

Your Privacy: Silhouette is committed to protecting your privacy. Our Privacy Policy is available online at www.eHarlequin.com or upon request from the Reader Service. From time to time we make our lists of customers available to reputable third parties who may have a product or service of interest to you. If you would prefer we not share your name and address, please check here. ☐

SSE09R

**Stay up-to-date
on all your romance
reading news!**

The Harlequin
Inside Romance
newsletter is a **FREE**
quarterly newsletter
highlighting
our upcoming
series releases
and promotions!

**Go to
eHarlequin.com/InsideRomance**
or e-mail us at
InsideRomance@Harlequin.com
to sign up to receive
your **FREE** newsletter today!

You can also subscribe by writing to us at: HARLEQUIN BOOKS
Attention: Customer Service Department
P.O. Box 9057, Buffalo, NY 14269-9057

Please allow 4-6 weeks for delivery of the first issue by mail.

IRNBPAQ209

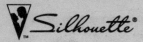

COMING NEXT MONTH

Available September 29, 2009

#1999 THE SHEIK AND THE BOUGHT BRIDE—
Susan Mallery
Famous Families/Desert Rogues
Prince Kateb intended to teach gold digger Victoria McCallen a lesson—he'd make her his mistress to pay off her dad's gambling debt! Until her true colors as a tender, caring woman raised the stakes—and turned the tables on the smitten sheik!

#2000 A WEAVER BABY—Allison Leigh
Men of the Double-C Ranch
Horse trainer J. D. Clay didn't think she could get pregnant—or that wealthy businessman Jake Forrest could be a loving daddy. But Jake was about to prove her wrong, offering J.D. and their miracle baby a love to last a lifetime.

#2001 THE NANNY AND ME—Teresa Southwick
The Nanny Network
Divorce attorney Blake Decker thought *he* had trust issues—until he met Casey Thomas, the nanny he hired for his orphaned niece. Casey didn't trust men, period. But anything could happen in such close quarters—including an attraction neither could deny or resist!

#2002 ACCIDENTAL CINDERELLA—
Nancy Robards Thompson
Take the island paradise of St. Michel, stir in scandalously sexy celebrity chef Carlos Montigo and voilà, down-on-her-luck TV presenter Lindsay Preston had all the ingredients for a new lease on life. And boy, was Carlos ever a dish….

#2003 THE TEXAS CEO'S SECRET—Nicole Foster
The Foleys and the McCords
With his family's jewelry store empire on the skids, Blake McCord didn't have time to dabble in romance—especially with his brother's former fiancée, Katie Whitcomb-Salgar. Or was the heiress just what the CEO needed to unlock his secret, sensual side?

#2004 DADDY ON DEMAND—Helen R. Myers
Left to raise twin nieces by himself, millionaire Collin Masters turned to his former—somewhat disgruntled—employee, Sabrina Sinclaire. She had no choice but to accept his job offer, and soon, his offer of love gave "help wanted" a whole new meaning….

SPECIAL EDITION